# LAST-MINUTE BRIDESMAID

"Let me check that I understand the deal," she whispered.

"One all-expenses-paid wedding, complete with bridesmaid duties, in exchange for two full days of your time as a business consultant. And you would be doing the actual number crunching—not some minion. Okay?"

Heath took her hand and pressed his long slender fingers around hers and held them tight just long enough for her to inhale his intoxicating scent. Combined with the texture of his smooth skin against hers as he slowly raised her hand to his lips and kissed the back of her knuckles, sensible thought became a tad difficult for a few seconds.

Because the moment his lips touched her skin, she was seventeen again and right back on her doorstep.

"Better than okay. It's a deal."

# DEAR READER,

Do you remember that high school St. Valentine dance when you were the only girl who turned up without a date?

Kate Lovat was rescued at the last minute by the stepbrother of her best friend Amber. Heath Sheridan is a gorgeous star university student and heir to the Sheridan publishing empire—and as far as Kate is concerned, the dreamiest date alive.

Now ten years later, it is Heath who needs the favor. Heath is the best man at his dad's third wedding and has just been dumped by his girlfriend. He needs a replacement bridesmaid in a hurry!

Handsome business executives, limos and manor houses— bring it on!

And where would Kate be without her very special friends? Amber, Kate and Saskia met up again at a high school reunion and are all back in London and all working hard to make new lives for themselves.

Saskia is still single and trying to stay sensible and in control, while Amber had been reunited with her teenage love, Sam. Look out for Saskia's story, which will be coming soon.

In the meantime I do hope that you enjoy Kate and Heath's journey to love and the happiness that they each deserve.

I am always delighted to hear from my readers and you can get in touch through my website at www. NinaHarrington.com.

Every best wish,

Nina

# LAST-MINUTE BRIDESMAID

NINA HARRINGTON

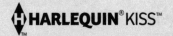

Recycling programs
for this product may
not exist in your area.

ISBN-13: 978-0-373-20727-5

LAST-MINUTE BRIDESMAID

Copyright © 2013 by Nina Harrington

www.Harlequin.com

# ABOUT NINA HARRINGTON

Nina grew up in rural Northumberland, England, and decided at the age of eleven that she was going to be a librarian—because then she could read *all* the books in the public library whenever she wanted! Since then she has been a shop assistant, community pharmacist, technical writer, university lecturer, volcano walker and industrial scientist, before taking a career break to realize her dream of being a fiction writer. When she is not creating stories that make her readers smile, her hobbies are cooking, eating, enjoying good wine—and talking, for which she has had specialist training.

**Other Harlequin® KISS™ titles by Nina Harrington:**

*The First Crush Is the Deepest*

This and other titles by Nina Harrington are available in ebook format—check out **www.Harlequin.com.**

———

# LAST-MINUTE BRIDESMAID

# PROLOGUE

———

*HIGH SCHOOL PARTIES were the worst punishment in the world! In fact, there should be a law banning them for all girls who had not managed to find a date—especially on Valentine's Day.*

Squeezing in between the gaggles of teenage girls who had formed a tight huddle on the other side of the dance floor, Kate Lovat clutched her empty plastic cola glass with both hands and tried to push her way through to the bar by waggling her hips and elbows.

It would be so much easier if she was a couple of inches taller!

Not even the high-heeled sandals she had bought in the January sales could bring her up to the shoulders of the posh clique of rich girl prefects who had made it their duty to take guard duty on the bar.

From this much sought-after position they could snigger and make snide comments about what every other girl at the sixth form school party was wearing or not wearing, who they had brought as their date and generally act superior in their designer mini dresses, which barely covered their gym-tight assets.

Kate had seen those assets in the school showers many times over the past three years and they still had the power to make her feel that she came from a different species of teenage girl. The kind that hated exercise and would rather eat her own feet than strut around the changing room in only a thong and heels, pretending to look for a hairdryer, which was Crystal Jardine's speciality.

Shame that Kate was providing them with such excellent entertainment.

So far the evening had been a disaster and she could not even rely on her pals to get her out of this one. Kate lifted her chin and tried to look around the crush of bodies to catch a glimpse of her backup crew.

Amber was laughing and chatting away with Sam in the corner, oblivious to anyone else in the room, Saskia was doing her best to entertain a girl cousin who had arrived from France the day before, and Petra was flirting with every boy in the room while her handsome date was at the bar. Nope. For once she was on her own.

'Kate...what a lovely dress,' Crystal simpered as she sneered down at her. 'It was so clever of you to find something second-hand suitable for a petite figure. Is that why you're the only girl in the class to turn up without a date on Valentine's? What a shame. After you've gone to *so* much effort to clean yourself up.'

A ripple of amused snorting ran around Crystal's little

band of followers, which had been dubbed the Crystal-lites by Saskia. Cold and transparent and all the same.

She couldn't help it. Kate had to run one hand down the side of her new strapless dark purple satin prom dress. She didn't have much in way of boobage or hips for a girl aged seventeen years and one month, but she had done what she could with the help of her friend Amber's bra collection. 'Oh, do you like the dress?' Kate looked up with an innocent expression and tried to fling off a casual reply. 'I designed it myself but I wasn't sure about the colour for my evening gloves.'

The tall blonde replied with a dismissive choke, 'Evening gloves? For a school disco? What era do you think this is? It's really embarrassing for the rest of us—in fact I suggest that you should take them off right now.' And with that she reached down and started pulling the sleeve of the glove down from Kate's elbow before she had time to snatch it away.

Kate gasped in disbelief and took a breath, ready to tell Crystal exactly what she could do with her suggestion, but before she had a chance to reply, four things happened in quick succession.

The plastic cola glass in her right hand fell, clattering, to the hard floor, Crystal blinked, pushed out her chest and did the hair-over-one-shoulder flick she reserved for full-on boy entrancement, the other girls in the group stopped yapping and started gawping and Kate instantly knew in every cell of her body, even before she turned around, that a very tall, very gorgeous man boy had just invaded their little world.

Her senses seemed to tune out the noise of the disco blasting out from the stage and the chatter that only forty teenage girls and their assorted friends and dates could make. It was as though she had been waiting all evening, no, all her life, to hear that rustling sound of crisp fabric and a rich aromatic aftershave which smelt of everything that represented old-school class, elegance, wealth and gorgeousness.

But she was still not prepared for the manly arm that wrapped around her waist and practically lifted her off her feet.

'Katherine, there you are. I've been looking for you everywhere.'

Kate half turned in the circle of his arms and slowly, hesitantly looked up into the face of the one and only Heath Sheridan.

Amber's stepbrother. Captain of the university polo team, heir to the Sheridan publishing empire, top of his business class, the celebrity party favourite, nice to children and animals.

And, to her, the most gorgeous twenty-year-old man *alive*.

He was smiling down at her with the full-on power smile she had seen him use before on the rare occasions that he came over to London from the Sheridan estate in Boston.

But she had never been on the receiving end of it up close and personal before. At this distance she could see the flecks of gold in those amazing dark brown eyes and the small scar on his smoothly shaven chin where, according to Amber, he had fallen off his sledge as a boy.

Well, that boy was long gone.

And hurrah and hallelujah and no complaints from her about that fact.

Heath's neat brown hair was clipped tight around his ears but just long enough at the back of his neck for her hand to touch as she raised both arms and linked them behind his head—just to lay it on extra-thick for the open-mouthed gawping audience, of course.

The fact that he instinctively slid both arms around her middle, forcing her to literally cling to his body, was a truly special bonus.

'Darling, you look wonderful,' Heath said, his gaze totally locked on her face. 'And that dress is divine on you. I am so sorry my flight was late getting into London. Can you ever forgive me?'

His voice was so husky, tinged with a soft transatlantic accent and deep and intimate that she could eat it with a spoon. It seemed to echo back in the small space that separated them, burning up the air and lodging inside her head, making her feel dizzy from lack of oxygen.

'Of course, Heath,' she replied in a low whisper. Her eyes fluttered closed for a second as her chest pressed against the open-necked silky white shirt he was wearing, which revealed just the smallest amount of chest hair but enough to do serious damage to her blood pressure, especially when his lips pressed into the top of her hair.

'Sorry, ladies,' he breathed, scarcely breaking his gaze to flick a look at Crystal, 'but I am going to have to steal my gorgeous girl away from you. We've been apart for far too long. Don't you agree, baby?'

A very unladylike squeak and part giggle escaped her lips and she managed a tiny self-satisfied but apologetic shoulder shrug as she slid back into her sandals, her feet hit the floor and she clung onto Heath's arm.

With a brilliant smile, his arm tightened around her waist, pulling her even tighter against his body and his lips met her forehead this time, claiming her in front of the entire posh clique, who were slowly moving from stunned shock to dagger-looks mode. As they moved away like some romantic three-legged race, Kate flicked her hair back and silently mouthed the words *elbow gloves* to the thunderous face of Crystal Jardine.

Two minutes later, Kate's feet had hardly touched the floor and she found herself standing propped up by Heath, next to Amber and Sam, who were smirking like mad—at her.

'How did I do, Kate?' Heath whispered in his very best husky voice into her ear, with his chin pressed against her temple. 'Do you think those girls got the message? Now why don't I get you that drink before I escort you all home?' Heath grinned and tipped up her chin with a cheeky wink. 'I take my job as a stand-in party date very seriously. So don't you dare go away. I'll be right back.'

She waited until Heath's hand had slid languorously down her arm and his back was turned before grabbing Amber by the arm and flicking her head towards the ladies' room.

'We'll just be a minute,' she absent-mindedly flung at

Sam, who simply shook his head, far too used to their little gang of rebels sticking together whenever possible. Petra seemed to have gone outside with a boy—typical—but Saskia didn't even have time to ask what was happening before Kate propelled her into the powder room and as far away as possible from the cubicles where most of the other girls in their class seemed to be either crying or noisily suffering the effects of cheap wine and vodka cocktails.

'What's the emergency? Has Crystal been winding you up again?' Saskia asked, trying not to shout above the ear-damaging background noise. 'I keep telling you that the girl is only jealous.'

Kate swept her two best pals into a tight huddle before taking a breath so that all of her words came out in one long rush. 'Heath Sheridan has just rescued me from the Crystallites and called me darling. And now he has gone to get me a drink. Amber, *help me out here. What shall I do*? I didn't think that Heath even knew my name!'

'Do?' the six-foot-tall stunning blonde replied with a laugh. 'You're asking the wrong person. He might be my stepbrother but Heath has always looked out for me. I say go with it and then accept his offer of a lift home. Your grandfather's place is just a few streets away and, from what I saw, he would be more than happy to see you home safely after he has dropped me off.'

'Safely? This is your Heath we are talking about here. You know, the boy who has his pick of the rich, gorgeous girls at university? And what about those celebrity mags you keep showing me? He always has some flash, sophisticated lady draped over him at some big cheese event or other. Boys like that don't have time for a seventeen-year-old wannabe fashion student.'

Saskia wrapped her arm around Kate's shoulder. 'Stop putting yourself down like that. You're gorgeous and he knows it. Top marks to Heath—and it's not as though he's a stranger. You have met him before and Amber adores him.'

Amber sniffed. 'I do. There is nobody else my mum would trust to deliver me home safe and sound—not even Sam. Go for it, Kate. He won't let you down. Be brave.'

Brave? Brave was fine when she was with her pals but it was a very different matter sitting in the passenger seat of Heath's sports car an hour later.

*Alone. With Heath Sheridan.*

Listening to his warm deep voice chatter on about the lecture he was planning to attend the next day. The radio was tuned to popular music, the brightly lit streets spun by and it seemed only minutes between leaving Amber's third dad's house and pulling up onto the pavement outside Kate's grandfather's shop. Her brain was spinning to come up with something clever and witty and eloquent to say. No chance! Breathing was hard enough, never mind talking.

Heath must think that she was a complete idiot. It was so humiliating.

And now he was opening the car door for her. If she was going to say something this was the time.

'Thank you, Heath,' she choked through a throat as

dry as the Sahara as she took his hand, locked her knees together and swung her legs out of the car with as much decorum as she could manage and lifted her chin. 'It was very kind of you to bring me home.'

His reply was to wrap one arm around her waist, push the car door closed with the other and half support her all of the four steps to the front door of the shop. Then wait until she had fished her key out of her tiny evening bag.

It was heaven and she sneaked a cuddle before he laughed out loud and whirled her around. 'You are most welcome, lovely lady. Any time.' And before she could reply he had lifted her gloved right hand to his lips and kissed the back of her knuckles. 'It was my pleasure.' He wrinkled his nose up and winked at her. And slowly, slowly, slid his hand from hers and half turned to go.

He was leaving. Heath was leaving. No!

Which was when she did it. Kate Lovat, doing-okay-but-not-likely-to-win-any-prizes high school student, trainee fashion designer and glove aficionado extraordinaire, stepped forward, grabbed the lapels of Heath's jacket with both hands, raised herself as high as she could on tiptoe, closed her eyes and kissed him on the mouth. *Hard.*

The startled and strangely delighted look on his face when she did squint her eyes open made her whirl around, turn the key in the door and hurl herself inside before she had to face him.

'Goodnight, Heath,' she whispered as she pressed her back to the door, heart thumping and lungs heaving. 'Goodnight. And very, very sweet dreams.'

# ONE

——

*Eleven years later.*

HEATH SHERIDAN WAS *going to kill her.*
He was going to jump up and stomp around and scowl and say that he knew that he had made a huge, huge mistake trusting her with something as important as making the bridesmaid dresses for his dad's wedding.

Kate Lovat lifted her left arm and squinted at her wristwatch for the tenth time in the last five minutes, then winced, sighed out loud and joggled from foot to foot.

Amber had warned her that Heath hated people being late to meetings. *Hated it.*

After all, he wasn't some heart-throb student any longer. Heath Sheridan was a serious publishing executive running his own media empire. He might have turned up late for that Valentine's Day dance, but this was different. This was business.

And she *was* now officially, undeniably, without doubt, late.

As in already ten minutes late. And that was allowing for the fact that her grandmother's watch always ran slow.

If only she hadn't bumped into Patrick, the friend she shared her loft with, on her way out.

Of course Pat wanted to check that he hadn't left anything behind in the studio, and then they'd got talking about his leaving party and then Leo had arrived to organise the photo shoot and…she'd finally escaped almost thirty minutes later. But it had always been the same. She was hopeless when it came to her friends.

*Simply hopeless.*

Just like her business management skills.

*Good thing that she was a goddess when it came to the actual tailoring.*

Kate slumped into the corner of the carriage of the rush-hour train on the London underground with both arms wrapped so tightly around her precious dress box that whenever the carriage lurched to one side, she lurched with it.

Today, of all days, the tube was slow leaving every single station on the route from her lowly design studio to the posh central London address for Sheridan Press. It seemed to be teasing her and the faster she willed it to go, the slower it went.

She had given up apologising to the other passengers after the first few times she had crashed into them and braced herself against the grubby glass partition instead.

The fact that she was too vertically challenged, as her friend Saskia called it, to reach the plastic loop swinging above her head was entirely immaterial when every lurch and rattle of the train seemed to be calling out in a sing-song tune the word *late,* rattle, *late, late,* rattle, *late.* Taunting her.

But it didn't matter. She had worked so hard on these dresses and they *were* lovely.

She would make Amber proud of her and prove to Heath and the wedding guests and their friends, hairdressers, postmen and anyone else they knew, how fabulously professional and creative she was and that they should choose Katherine Lovat Designs to create all of their future outfits.

With a bit of luck this wedding would be exactly the type of promotional opportunity she had been looking for. The first three dresses had already been delivered to the bride and the fourth and final dress had been finished right on deadline. Just as she had promised it would be.

Now all she had to do was go out into a thunderstorm and deliver the final dress—and she would be done.

Kate glanced down at her damp high-heeled peep-toe ankle boots and crunched her toes together several times to get the circulation going again.

Okay, maybe they weren't the most sensible footwear in the world for trudging through city streets on the way to make a special delivery, but it shouldn't be raining in July. It should be sunny and warm and the pavements dry enough to walk on without being in danger of being drenched from passing cars.

The train slowed but Kate's pulse started to race as she peered out at the curved tile walls as they pulled into the tube station.

This was it. She swallowed down a lump of anxiety and nervous tension the size of a wedding hat, and then she lifted her chin and turned on her trademark bright and breezy happy smile.

*Nothing to see here, folks. Move along. Everything is fine in Kate land.*

*No problems at all.*

The lease on the warehouse studio which she rented with Patrick had *not* just doubled in cost in the last year, Patrick had *not* just decided to leave London and move to Hollywood as a wardrobe assistant in the movie business and, biggest of all, she was totally, absolutely *not* nervous about meeting the man she was on her way to see at that minute.

Heath Sheridan was Amber's ex-stepbrother. That was all. And her silly teenage crush was over years ago!

So what if she had pounced on Heath the last time that she had seen him? They had both kissed a lot of other people since then. He was bound to have forgotten that embarrassing little incident...wouldn't he?

She had never seen Heath since that night and he certainly hadn't got in touch with her. But of course that was the autumn his mother had been taken ill and coming back to London wasn't included in his plans.

No. This was a straightforward business transaction. Heath needed the last of the four bridesmaids' dresses today and was willing to pay extra to have it delivered in person.

Why should it matter if Heath saw her looking like a

drowned rat? With her soggy bare toes sticking out of her damp designer boots?

He probably wouldn't even notice that she was late for their meeting. *And wet.*

*Probably.*

And if he did, well, she could simply make a joke of her problems. The way she always did.

The glass doors slid open behind her back and Kate exploded onto the crowded platform with the crush of other passengers behind her with such momentum that she had to press one hand against the wall to protect her precious cargo.

And instantly winced.

She had just touched a wall decorated with graffiti, and who knew what else, with her white lace summer gloves.

*Well, this day was getting better all the time.*

It would actually be funny if she wasn't so nervous.

She sucked in a breath of hot fuel and soot-filled air charged with that tang of electricity from the tracks.

*Nervous?* Kate Lovat did not do nervous.

Kate Lovat was brave and strong and invincible and courageous.

Kate Lovat was going to exude an aura of total confidence and professionalism and Heath's family would recommend her work to all of their friends.

Kate Lovat had just spent an hour on her make-up so that it looked natural, and much longer choosing a professional outfit which would impress even the toughest of clients.

She clutched the dress box to her chest as she boarded the escalator.

She needed high-profile clients like the Sheridans to adore the bridesmaids' dresses she had created. After all, she had followed the brief Heath had emailed her to the letter.

Okay. Maybe she might have added *a little* something extra. After all, she had to stamp some Lovat flourish on her work. Otherwise, what would be the point of making something unique?

A smile crept up from her mouth to her eyes and a quick chuckle caught in her throat.

Watch out, Heath Sheridan. *Ready or not, here I come. Get ready to be dazzled.*

'The trade fair figures are not what we wanted, Heath. The presentations were brilliant and every buyer I spoke to was impressed with the quality of the hardbacks, but they are dragging their heels when it comes to firm orders,' Lucas explained, his exasperation clear even down the cellphone from a Malaysian hotel. 'The book stores simply don't want to hold a wide range of reference titles which only shift a few copies a year.'

Heath Sheridan scanned through the sales figures that had arrived onto his notebook computer in the past few minutes and quickly pulled together a comparison chart of how book sales were tracking in each region.

No matter how he mapped the data, the results were the same.

Sales were down in every category of reference book

that had made Sheridan Press one of the few remaining commercially successful privately owned international publishing houses. The company had made its name one hundred and twenty years ago with high end, beautifully produced reference books. Biographies, dictionaries and atlases. Lovely books designed to last. And they did last. And that was the problem.

Over the past few weeks he had worked with Lucas and his talented marketing team to come up with a brilliant promotional campaign which focused on how Sheridan Press had invested in digital technology to illustrate the books which were still bound by hand so that every single reference book was a unique work of art. A superb combination of the latest technology with the finest hand-crafting techniques that four generations of the Sheridan family had created.

Shame that the booksellers did not see it that way.

That was precisely the kind of approach that his father had been looking for when he'd asked Heath to inject some new blood into the company—and save the jobs of hundreds of employees who made up Sheridan Press in the process.

Growing up, he had spent more time watching men embossing gold letters onto beautiful books than he had watching sports. These men had given their lives to the Sheridan family, just as their fathers and grandfathers had done before them.

He could not fail them. He would not fail them.

Heath exhaled long and slow before replying to his father's Far East sales manager, who had lost just as much sleep as he had preparing for this sales trip. 'I know that you and your team did the very best you could, Lucas—thank you for all of your hard work,' Heath said, trying to inject a lighter tone to his voice. 'Let's see what Hong Kong brings! I can just see all of those new undergraduates heading off to university with some Sheridan books under their arms this fall.'

'Absolutely.' Lucas laughed out loud. 'Call you when we get there. Oh—and don't forget to take some time out to enjoy yourself at the wedding of the year. I'm glad I don't have to come up with a best man's speech for my own dad.'

'Hey! I'm going to be a great best man. But, talking about enjoying yourself—why not take the team out to celebrate on Saturday? I'll pick up the tab.'

'Sounds good to me. Call you later in the week.'

The cellphone clicked off, leaving Heath in silence, his quick brain working through the ramifications of the call. Frustration and exasperation combined with resigned acceptance. This promotional tour of the Far East book fairs had to pay for itself in increased sales. This was precisely the market the investment in new technology was designed to attract.

He had been convinced that the techniques that had worked so brilliantly in the commercial fiction line of the Sheridan publishing empire, could be applied to the reference book section. He had taken over a tiny and neglected division straight out of university and transformed it into one of the seven top commercial publishers in the world. The profits from Sheridan Media had been keeping Sheridan Press afloat for years.

Surely it was time to reap the benefits of ten years of driving himself with a punishing workload. When was the last time that he had a holiday? And what about the series of failed relationships and missed family events?

There had to be a way to use all of that hard-won success to save the reference books. And save his relationship with his father at the same time.

His father had reached out to ask for his business advice. It was a small step—but a real step. And an important one in rebuilding their fragile family life. The media loved it and Heath had set up press releases and interviews which had rippled through the publishing world. New technology and traditional craftsmanship. Father and son. It was a golden ticket. Heath Sheridan was the equivalent of calling in the cavalry to save yet another much respected publisher from going to the wall.

He had jumped at the chance, excited by the possibilities. And excited by the opportunity to spend more time with Charles Sheridan. They had never had an easy-going relationship and this was the first time they had worked together as professionals.

Of course he hadn't counted on being asked to be best man at his own father's wedding. Especially considering who the bride was. That was an unexpected twist.

Asking for help or acknowledging any kind of problem had never been Charles Sheridan's strong point. Maybe he should report back on what Lucas had told him.

Heath flipped open his phone when there was a polite

cough and he looked up, blinking. The car had pulled to a halt and his driver was standing on the pavement, holding the door open for him while the rain soaked into the shoulders of his smart jacket.

Apologising profusely, Heath generously tipped the driver and stepped out of the executive car his father had sent to collect him from the airport. He stood long enough to take one quick glance up at the elegant stone building that was now the London office of Sheridan Press before the reporters realised who he was and ran out from the shelter of the arched entrance, cameras flashing.

Heath pulled his coat closer as protection against the heavy rain and smiled at the press.

Dealing with the media was all part of the job—as long as they produced column inches in the financial and trade press, then he was happy.

'*Mr Sheridan. Over here, sir. Mr Sheridan, is it true that you are taking over Sheridan Press when your father retires, Mr Sheridan?*'

'*What can you tell us about rumours that the printing operation is going overseas, Mr Sheridan?*'

'*How do you feel about being the best man at your father's wedding? Is it third time lucky for Charles Sheridan?*'

'Thanks for coming out in this typically English summer weather, everyone.' Heath smiled and waved at the cameras before turning to the female reporter who had asked the last question. 'Alice Jardine is a lovely lady who my father has known for many years as a close friend. I wish them every happiness together. Of course I was delighted when my father asked me to be the best man at his wedding this weekend—it isn't often that happens. As for the company? Business as usual, ladies and gentlemen. And no closures. Not while I am on the team. Thank you.'

And at that, by some unspoken signal, the main entrance doors slid open and Heath stepped inside with a quick smile and a wave.

But, just as he turned away from the press, a man's voice echoed from over his shoulder, 'Is it true that your late mother and Alice Jardine were good friends, Mr Sheridan? How do you feel about that?'

The doors slid shut and Heath carried on walking across the pale marble floor of the hallway, apparently deaf to the question, and it was only in the solitary space of the elevator that he slowly unclenched his fingers.

One by one. Willing each breath he took to slow down as the words of that last question repeated over and over again inside his head.

*Feel?*

*How did he feel about the fact that the woman who had been his mother's best friend was marrying his father?*

*How did he feel about the fact that Alice had been with his father while his mother lay dying in a hospice?*

*How did he feel?*

Heath tugged hard at the double cuffs of his tailor-made shirt and fought back the temptation to hit something hard.

But that wouldn't fit into his carefully designed image.

Heath Sheridan did not get ruffled or upset or display outrageous bursts of emotion and temper. Oh, no.

He played it cool. He was a Boston Sheridan and the Boston Sheridans kept their feelings buried deep enough to be icebergs.

Well, this ice man was not going to melt and let the rest of the world feel the heat of the raging temper that was burning inside him at that moment, threatening to spill out into some ill-judged outburst.

So what if his father's choice of bride hit one of his hot buttons?

He could deal with it. Was dealing with it. Would continue to deal with it.

Ironic that he should be asked that question outside the very house where his mother had spent the first twenty years of her life. The house had been built for his grandparents, who had been part of a group of aristocratic artist writers and intellectuals in the Arts and Crafts movement in the nineteen-thirties and the Art Deco features were original and stunning, especially in the library. Two storeys of hand-carved teak shelves were connected by a circular staircase which led onto an upper-level gallery, lit by a central domed roof.

Of course it had the wow factor for visitors to Sheridan Press, who were too much in awe to take notice of the fact that the recent catalogue of Sheridan books would fit neatly into one small part of the lower shelf.

Heath remembered playing hide-and-seek in the many stunning rooms, attics and cellars when he was a boy on rare visits to London with his parents, but now it was little more than a private meeting venue for his father and his circle of artist friends like Alice Jardine.

Closing his eyes, he could almost see his mother playing the piano in the drawing room below while he played with his grandparents in the patio garden outside the open French windows. The smell of lavender and beeswax. Old books and linseed oil. Because, above everything else, this house had always been filled with artists, the dinner table chatter was about art, the library full of books and exhibition catalogues about art and, of course, every available wall had been a living, constantly changing art gallery.

The thought of Alice walking these corridors where his mother had been so very happy was something that he was slowly coming to terms with. But he wasn't there yet. And he wasn't entirely sure that he ever would be.

That was something else he was going to have to work on.

In the meantime? He had a wedding to survive. A wedding where it was going to be crucial to pretend that all was rosy in the Sheridan family, and father and son were working together like the dream team they were pretending to be.

Heath strolled over to the lovely polished marquetry desk and sat down heavily on an antique chair, which creaked alarmingly at the weight.

His father and his new fiancée had ordered a relaxed country house wedding—and that was precisely what they were going to get—with his help.

Heath opened up his laptop and was just about to dive into the checklist for the wedding arrangements when his cellphone rang and he flipped it open and answered without even checking to see who was calling him.

'Sheridan,' he said, and jammed the phone between his solid wide jaw and his shoulder blade so that he could scroll down the project plan and highlight the key activities while taking the call at the same time.

'Heath? Heath, is that you?' a female voice called down the worst phone line that he had ever heard. Loud crackling noises and what sounded like thunder screamed out at him.

Heath instantly focused on the call. 'Olivia, I was starting to get worried. Did you make your flight to London on time? Sorry about the British weather but the forecast is looking good for the next few days.'

The response was a loud clattering sound as though heavy objects were being dropped onto a metal floor, and Heath held the phone a few inches away from his ear until he heard his girlfriend's voice, which gradually became clearer. 'That's what I've been trying to tell you, but all the lines are down. I'm still in China. Heath?'

He closed his eyes and counted to ten before blinking. 'Olivia, tell me that you're joking.'

'The tropical storm that hit three days ago has just been declared a typhoon,' her echoing voice replied. 'A typhoon! Would you believe it? Even the helicopters have been grounded.'

Heath pinched the top of his nose, and then quickly typed in search details for the weather in Southern China. Whirls of thick white cloud and misty shapes of land masses covered with warning symbols reflected back at him from the screen as he replied. 'This looks serious. Are you okay? I mean, do you have somewhere safe to go until the weather clears?'

'The valley has already flooded,' she yelled, 'so the whole team is being evacuated further up the mountain into the cave system.' Then she paused for a second. 'I have to be honest with you, Heath. Even if the weather had been good, I had already decided not to fly to London for your father's wedding.'

Tension creased his brow as Heath tabbed though the images and he slumped back in the hard chair. 'What do you mean? We talked about this a few weeks ago,' he replied and clasped the fingers of one hand around the back of his neck and rubbed it back and forth as a cold hollow feeling pooled in the pit of his stomach.

'No. You talked. And I tried to explain that I needed time away on my own to think about where our relationship was heading. It's been almost a year now, Heath, and you are just as cold and guarded as you were the day I first met you. Your work is more important than me. Than us. I'm sorry, Heath, but I can't keep this relationship alive on my own. I think it is better if we go our separate ways. I want something more. We both deserve a chance for happiness. And mine is not with you.'

She seemed about to say something when muffled voices and engine noise echoed down the phone. 'I have to go. Please send Charles and Alice my apologies and tell them I'll catch up the minute I get back. I'll be thinking of you this weekend and we'll talk more when I get back.

And I am sorry, Heath, but this is goodbye. Have a great time at the wedding. Bye.'

And then the phone went dead.

Heath Sheridan stared at the completely innocent telephone for several seconds while he suppressed the urge to throw it out of the stained-glass window.

*This is goodbye? Have a great time at the wedding?*

*What had just happened? Because, unless he had completely got it wrong...his girlfriend had just broken up with him. On the telephone. From China.*

Okay. It was July and this would have been the first time that they had spent more than a couple of days together since New Year. He had frantically completed a major promotional tour for his bestselling thriller author before moving to Boston to work for Sheridan Press. There never seemed to be enough hours in the day, especially over the past few months.

*And what about her work?*

Olivia's anthropology project with Beijing University had turned into a major excavation into cave art which would take years to complete. She had even had to send the dressmaker her dimensions for her bridesmaid's dress by email. He knew this because he was the one who had taken the barrage of complaints from Kate Lovat about making a bridesmaid's dress for a slim five-foot-three girl who would have to wear the dress without a single fitting.

Heath's fingers froze on the keyboard.

*Oh, no.*

He was going to have to tell the bride that she was going to have to walk down the aisle of the village church on her family estate with three bridesmaids instead of four.

He dropped his head into his hands and groaned.

*He was toast.*

# TWO

---

KATE STOOD IN the doorway to the library room and took a breath.

The last time that she had seen Heath Sheridan was at a high school dance and it had certainly been a memorable occasion. Just thinking about that moment when she had jumped on him to say goodnight made her feel so embarrassed and intimidated. And that was without the height difference, which meant that he towered over her without even trying.

Kate shrugged off her nerves. That was years ago. This time they were equal. Two professionals with their own businesses.

Unfortunately for her poor heart, Heath Sheridan had the nerve to have actually become even more handsome than the man she remembered and Amber talked about constantly.

The star student who had made his name turning around the popular fiction division of the family publishing company should be round-shouldered and wear cardigans with leather patches at the elbow.

He had no right to be so tall and clear-skinned. And that hair! Lush dark brown hair which curled into the base of his neck and seemed to have a mind of its own. He had never been vain—she knew that from talking to Amber—but style and vanity were two very different matters and Heath Sheridan had style to spare.

Why shouldn't he?

Amber wore gowns by top fashion houses and his family were on the top level of Boston society. It made perfect sense for him to be wearing a tailored black suit and shirt which fitted him so perfectly she knew instinctively that they had been made to measure.

Those strong shoulders, slim waist and hips would be a gift to any tailor.

*Oh, my. And how she would like to dress him.*

Suddenly the room become stiflingly hot and it had nothing to do with the weather!

'Ah! There you are,' Kate called out through a tight throat. 'Special delivery for the man of the house, courtesy of Lovat courier services. Great to see you again, Heath.'

She waited for him to turn around and give her one of those fabulous grins that used to make her teenage knees wobble.

And she waited. And then she waited a little longer. But his gaze stayed totally locked onto whatever he was finding so fascinating on his computer screen. She could see that he was reading and typing so he was not asleep.

So she tried again.

'Hi, Heath. Your one-woman dressmaker and delivery service is here.'

Kate looked at Heath and then looked at the pretty dress box that she had slaved for hours to create and then carted across London in a downpour.

She might forgive him for not turning around to greet her but there was no way that he was going to ignore the fabulous work that she had done.

'*Thank you, Kate. You were such a star to drop everything else that you were working on to create four amazing outfits at the very last minute as a personal favour,*' she murmured under her breath as she slung her shoulder bag higher over her shoulder.

'*Sorry I cannot find the time to even look at your work,*' she added with a mock lilt in her voice. '*Don't let the door swing on your way out.*'

Heath did not even glance at her.

Right. Well, that answered that question. 'Bye, Heath. See you around some time. Have a fabulous wedding. The bill is in the post.'

Still no reply.

*What had she been thinking?*

The fashion design company she had created from scratch and passion was in so much trouble. She should be back in her studio working on ballet costumes for her pal Leo, not spending what little free time she had stolen from the day getting dressed up to deliver wedding clothes as a favour for her friend's stepbrother.

Her friend's gorgeous, handsome, debonair and totally oblivious to the fact that she existed brother.

She was delusional. And more than a little pathetic.

'Have a lovely wedding. I do hope everything goes well. Why don't I just leave this last dress with you and call you later? Bye!' she smiled and sang out in a sing-song voice.

*Nothing. Not even a raised eyebrow.*

Kate pressed a hand to each hip. *Well, now he was just being rude.*

Kate tossed her bag onto a chair and stomped over to the desk and, before Heath could do anything to stop her, closed the lid down on his laptop and swivelled the chair away from the desk.

And at that very moment he looked up and turned his head.

His mouth twisted into a half smile that screamed out that he had known that she was there the whole time. Eyes the colour of the burnt sugar coating on the top of a crème caramel dessert smiled at her, dazzling and driving any chance of sensible thought from her brain.

She half closed her eyes and scowled at him then rapped her knuckles twice on his forehead. Hard.

'Hello. Is anyone at home?' she said, ignoring his shouts of protest. 'Remember me? The girl who has just gone out of her way to hand-deliver the last bridesmaid's dress so that your new stepmum won't be followed down the aisle by a girl in cargo pants?'

'Kate. Yes. Of course. How long have you been waiting?' Heath replied with a groan as he rubbed life back into his forehead.

'Long enough to realise that you have not been listening to a word that I have said. In fact a person of delicate sensibilities might even call you rude and insulting.'

'Oh, no. Did I just zone out on you?'

She nodded slowly, up and down, her lips pushed forward. 'If that is what you call totally ignoring me for the past five minutes, then yes, you did.'

Then he did the smiley thing again and there was just enough of a twinkle in those eyes to drive away the clouds.

*Wow, some men just ticked all the boxes. It was so unfair to the others.*

'I apologise. It is one of my many flaws and I had no intention of being rude or ignoring you. I spend most of my time in an open-plan publishing office with a team who are never off the phone. Being able to disconnect is actually an advantage. But not always.'

She leant back and scowled at him, 'Really?'

'Really,' he whispered, and the corners of his mouth turned up into a small smile. 'I do that a lot when I'm stressed. And I am stressed. This wedding is driving me crazy. Am I forgiven?'

'I'm thinking about it,' she retorted. 'Well, that is such a pathetic excuse, but I suppose that it will have to do. But why is this wedding driving *you* crazy? Are you thinking of leaving the publishing world behind to retrain as a wedding planner?'

His eyes closed and he gave a pretend dramatic shudder. 'I don't know how they do it. This was supposed to be a small family wedding. Low-key. Intimate. You would think that it would be easy to manage. Think again.' He raked both hands back through his hair and her breathing rate went up a notch just at the sight of it.

'So why are you helping to organise this wedding?'

'Family, duty. And the fact that my dad asked me to be his best man just when he was supposed to be in the middle of launching a new publishing line in Britain. It was only when I started asking questions that it soon became apparent that the whole event was in need of serious organisation.'

He shook his head. 'Artists and writers are so talented, but their focus isn't usually on the minute details. The bride's cousin offered to make all of the arrangements as her—' and at this he made inverted commas with his fingers '—wedding present to the happy couple. I thought that my mum's family were bad enough but the Jardines have taken chaos to the next level.'

'Hey. I'm an artist. And we can be organised when we have to be!'

Heath Sheridan swivelled around in the heavy leather chair and gave his full attention to the pint-sized bundle of brightness and fun and energy who had burst into the hallowed library.

And then looked twice. Then looked again.

The girl standing looking at him in the elegant grey business suit had Kate's voice but she had certainly changed a lot from the fashion student with wild hair and wilder clothing who he vaguely remembered as one of Amber's school friends.

Her layered short brown hair framed delicate features and a pair of clear, determined and very green eyes. A sprinkle of summer freckles covered her nose but her eyes and lips had been expertly made up to make her features look magical in the diffuse light of the library.

Kate Lovat was a pixie in a skirt suit.

She seemed taller than he recalled from their last meeting but then he was sitting down and she was wearing...what was she wearing on her feet? Platform stiletto boots—but the front had been cut away so that her toes stuck out.

Why would anyone wear ankle boots—which were open-toed?

There had to be some logical explanation but at that moment he could not think of a single one, except that, oh yes—the quirky Kate was still there under the slick make-up and suit.

'Organised? I'm very pleased to hear it,' he coughed, quickly trying to drag his gaze away from her legs, 'because that would make two of us. My father wanted the wedding to go smoothly. So there was only one thing for me to do—take control of the arrangements as my gift to my dad. It's a different sort of wedding present, but at least it saves on wrapping paper.'

'Ah. Control.' She smiled and gave a small shoulder wiggle, which acted like a shot of warmth in the cool room. 'Now I'm getting the picture. Well, now you can relax because I have something special for you. The last of the bridesmaids' dresses. I finished it this morning and it is fabulous—' she paused and looked up from unwrapping a long thick card box and gave a small shrug '—of course—' then went back to untying the ribbons and lifting off the lid '—so you can relax and tick that off your list. They are all done. And, what's more, you have a chance to check the merchandise before the bride. Now that is an opportunity not to be missed. But clean hands only. No sticky paws.'

*Sticky paws? What?*

Heath closed the distance between them and leant down to peer inside the card box, which seemed to be filled with sheets of silky cream tissue paper.

Kate's tailored pale grey and white tweed jacket hung open at the front, revealing a coral-coloured stretchy-looking top which clung to her curves above a slim matching grey pencil skirt.

She might be wearing high-heeled shoes but she still only came up to his shoulder. A floral fragrance of roses, gardenias and jasmine filled his head. She smelt of summer on a wet and windy day and suddenly his world seemed a happier place. *How did she do that?*

'I have to admit,' she continued and slipped away from his touch, 'I am always happy to make personal deliveries to my customers, but you did cut it fine.'

He paused and glanced out of the window before strolling across to the fine wooden cabinet with a hidden refrigerator inside and picking out two bottles of water and two glasses. 'Last-minute decision. What do you give the bride who already has everything?'

'Um. Good point. A toaster wouldn't exactly cut it. I mean...' she turned her head from side to side as though to check that they were alone '...I take it that the bride is not some flighty gold-digger after your dad's loot.'

The water caught in his throat and went down the wrong way, making him cough and splutter over his computer. Kate stood on tiptoe to thump him hard between the shoulder blades. Twice. Until he lifted his hand in submission and turned back to her. After a couple of deep breaths he blinked and wiped tears from the corners of his eyes, well aware that Kate's gaze was locked onto his face.

'Thank you,' he wheezed. 'And no. Alice is definitely not after my dad for his money. She was the one who wanted a family wedding at the Jardine country estate. She knows how my dad hates fuss. This suits him very well and I'm happy to help make it all go smoothly.'

'Are you in training for Amber's wedding?' She nodded. 'What? Why are you shaking your head like that?'

'Because there is no way that I ever want to do this again. Once is quite enough. You have no idea of the things I have had to deal with. And just wait until Alice and my dad get back from the airport with the last batch of guests. You do not want to be here when I break the news about Olivia.'

Kate reared back with a puzzled look on her face. 'Olivia? What news about Olivia?'

Heath pressed a finger and thumb into the bridge of his nose.

*What news? How about the fact that my girlfriend has just decided to dump me days before my father's wedding? That's all. Because apparently I am cold and guarded. Noth-*

*ing important. Nothing to worry about. Just one more relationship down the pan.*

He closed his eyes for a second in a futile attempt to regain control. But Olivia's words kept echoing through his brain until they were all he could think about.

*Cold and guarded.*

This was pretty much the same thing the two girlfriends before Olivia had complained about. Was he cold? Guarded, yes. He did protect himself from becoming emotionally dependent on anyone, and especially a woman. Why shouldn't he? He had seen the massive damage that kind of relationship could have on the family and the man. There was no way that he could ever allow himself to love one person and one place so completely. Not when they could be snatched away from him at a moment's notice and he was powerless to prevent it. But cold?

Blinking his eyes open, Heath was about to reply to Kate's question with some casual throwaway comment, when his gaze fell on the open box.

Something sparkling and shiny nestled in the tissue paper.

In two steps he was standing, looking in disbelief at the confection of dusty pink lace and satin, scarcely able to believe his eyes.

'What's this?' he asked, pointing to the swirls of iridescent ivory-coloured pearls which had been sewn into the lacework across the bodice and sleeves.

'Embellishment, of course.' She grinned.

He should have known that things were going too smoothly. Embellishment!

Amber had trusted Kate, but then again Amber adored her friends and was obviously incapable of being objective about their abilities.

After today's little bombshell from Olivia, the last thing he wanted to do was deal with faulty bridesmaids' dresses.

Heath picked up his tablet computer and scanned through emails. 'Alice sent me very specific instructions about the bridesmaids' dresses that she required for her wedding. All four had to be the same design and made of the same fabric. Very plain. And no mention of the word embellishment.'

He looked up at her, eyebrows raised. 'Has she made any comments about the first three?'

Kate nodded. 'Alice has been travelling with your father for the past two weeks so I sent them over to the Manor yesterday. She texted me to say that they had arrived safe and sound but she wasn't going to open the boxes until her bridesmaids arrived.'

'So Alice hasn't checked the dresses yet.'

'What? And spoil the fun of opening the boxes with the gals? It will be like Christmas morning.'

'Right. All I asked you to do, Kate, was make four very plain dresses. That was simple enough, wasn't it?' His gaze focused on the beaded neckline. 'I didn't think that you would change the design into something more elaborate.'

'You're forgetting something very important.' She glared at him. 'People pay me to transform a simple idea into a beautiful design. Otherwise why bother having dresses made-to-measure? Alice could have gone to a department store for a plain dress. She expects me to do something creative with this idea. Don't you like the idea of being creative?'

Creative? He had grown up with an artist mother whose idea of responsibility was making sure there was always paint and canvas in the house. Everything else was unnecessary. Timetables were for other people to follow, not her. She was talented, celebrated, enchanting and, for a teenage boy desperate for some structure in his life, totally exasperating.

Kate Lovat was clearly cut from the same mould.

Not even an elegant grey and white pinstripe skirt suit could hide the fact that she was just as irresponsible and creative as the girl he remembered from the last time they'd met.

He should have guessed that Kate had not changed that much. Who else would choose to wear quirky red leather ankle boots with her toes sticking out the front on a wet July afternoon?

His gaze scanned her legs—and lingered a little too long on those shapely smooth legs before focusing on the footwear. Her toenails were painted in the exact same shade of red as her boots.

Fire engine red.

A flaming symbol of her attitude to life.

Well, it certainly fitted, because she had just managed to spark a match under the very last scrap of patience he had held on to for emergencies and burnt it to a crisp.

There was one thing he hated above anything else—and that was surprises.

'Are all four dresses like this one?' he asked with a rock-stiff jaw.

'Of course they are. You ordered matching outfits.'

A deep furrow appeared between Heath's brows and the air practically crackled with electricity as he exploded with a reply. 'Kate, Alice ordered plain. I don't know much about fashion, but this is not plain.'

Kate stepped forward so that her entire body was only inches away from his, and the fire in her eyes was the same colour as her toenails.

'And I know about fashion. Alice. *Will love*. These dresses. The bridesmaids *will love* these dresses. Your father *will love* these dresses. The entire clan gathered for this shindig will love these dresses. And the wedding will be a huge success, Heath. Job done.'

'Job done? I don't think so. Have you any idea how important this wedding is? This is the first time in ten years that my father's asked me to do anything for him. I'm not prepared to see their wedding day ruined by you taking creative licence. These dresses will have to be altered.'

Concern fuelled his anger but Kate's response threw petrol onto the flames.

Because she did not look away or back down. She stared him out, and the look in her eyes was something new, something he had not seen before.

This was not the same girl he remembered. Little Kate had certainly grown up.

'Change them? Do you have any idea what you are saying?' Her words came out in a staccato retort of crisp clear sounds as though she was struggling to contain herself. 'There is no way that I can alter even one of these dresses before the weekend. So, as far as I am concerned, this is it. No negotiation. No replacements.'

A surge of disbelief swept through him and he was about to launch into a tirade when his cellphone rang. His personal assistant was returning his call.

'Don't go anywhere,' he ordered, pointing the phone at her chest like a baton and turned back to the desk and the sales figures.

Kate desperately fought to find the words needed to frame some kind of response but was saved when he moved out of earshot.

With a twist of her heels she turned away from him and leapt back up the stairs and tugged open the glass cases that held the books and pretended to be fascinated in the first book she picked up.

Her eyes were too blurry to read the title on the spine or admire the fine end papers.

The one thing that she had been secretly dreading for years had finally happened.

She wasn't good enough for Heath.

And he had no idea whatsoever of how much pain and humiliation she felt at a few simple words of condemnation.

He was rejecting this dress that she had worked on for hour after hour of painstaking hand-sewing after a few seconds of his so very precious time. How could he not know that when he rejected her work he was reject-ing her and everything she stood for and had worked for at the same time?

Time and time again she had come up against the same attitude, the same complaint, and the same de-mand. Keep it simple. Don't get clever. Conform to what everyone else is doing. That way we might like you and take you seriously.

Even her own parents thought that she should con-form. Sacrifice her creativity and ideas on the altar of the bland and the stale and the conventional.

And just the thought of that made her heart shrink with pain and anguish.

She had always known that Heath would be different, but facing it head-on in a stark announcement like this was a lot harder than she had expected. The pain hit her just behind the knees and she casually flicked her skirt out and sat down on the step before she fell down and felt even more of a fool.

She had to get out of here.

That was it.

She had made her delivery. Her job was done.

The moment her legs started working again she could take off back to the studio and lock the door and laugh about what a silly teenage crush she had once upon a time on a man who turned out to be not worth it after all.

*This was so totally crazy it was mad.*

Heath had never looked on her as anything else than Amber's funny little school friend. Someone he had never taken seriously. Someone he humoured because he loved Amber and wanted to make her happy.

Part of her respected that.

Shame that the rest of her wanted to get home as fast as she could and cry her heart out over a bucket of ice cream.

This was not just futile but ridiculous and pathetic. She had finally had the rose-tinted spectacles whipped from her eyes so that she could see Heath for who he was and not the boy she had kissed on her doorstep all of those years ago.

Strange. She should be used to being disappointed with men, but she had always hoped that Heath would be different. That he would be the caring man that Amber adored.

She had dated fashion designers, artists and musicians who all claimed to be creative and experimental—but in the end they all turned out to be bland and conformist, too willing to change their ideas to fit in, and she had walked away from every one of them.

Hoping for something better. Hoping for someone who liked her exactly the way she was and loved what she did and did not want to change her or 'shape her talent' as one agent had called it.

No, thanks. She decided what she did. She set the standards and followed her dream and nobody, not even Heath, was going to stop her from keeping her fashion designs alive.

No. She would stay as she was. Amber's little friend. That way, Heath would never know how much effort it took for her to get back to her feet and look at him cross-ing the room through the raging sea of confused emo-tions and regret that were still roiling inside her.

'Fine,' she replied, and folded the tissue paper over the dress, closed down the lid on the box and popped it under her arm before staring up into his face with a clear serious expression. 'I'll take this dress. But you have to understand something. This might be your father's third marriage, Mr Sheridan. But this will be my fifteenth. Yes, that's right; so far fourteen brides have trusted me to be creative with their wedding garments and by the end of the season that will be twenty.'

She took a tight hold of the box, which seemed out-rageously large compared to her tiny frame. 'You know where to find me if you change your mind. Good luck on the big day. You're going to need it. Because right now your precious girlfriend Olivia doesn't have a bridesmaid dress—and try explaining that to the bride. End of.'

And with that she turned on her heel and walked straight out of the door, her hips swaying, her high-heeled boots clicking on the hardwood floor and her seriously annoyed nose high in the air.

# THREE

———

HEATH SHERIDAN STEPPED out from the back seat of the black London cab, tugged down his suit jacket, then turned and thanked the driver. The taxi slid away from the kerb, leaving him standing on the pavement outside Kate's studio feeling rather like a teenager watching his parents drive away from his boarding school on the first morning of the new term.

He knew that feeling only too well and it nagged at the deep well of disquiet before he rolled his shoulders back and strolled out into the bright July sunshine.

An imposing two-level stone warehouse stretched out the whole length of one side of the cobbled street. It reminded him very much of the Sheridan print works back in an old part of Boston which had not changed over the last one hundred years. Impressive buildings like these were created to intimidate visitors with the power and wealth of the owners in a time before press conferences and the kind of celebrity TV interviews he was accustomed to organizing for his bestselling fiction writers.

Well, he knew all about that. Sheridan Press had built up a reputation through years of hard work and quiet, understated excellence. Not flashy promotions or grand gestures. That was the world that his father had grown up in, which made it even more remarkable that he had swallowed his pride and asked Heath to help him.

In hindsight he should have guessed that there was more to the request than the business problems—but he had never expected it to be personal.

Just one more reason why Alice Jardine was going to have four bridesmaids walking behind her on Saturday, not three.

A passing delivery van snapped Heath awake and he straightened his back and strode towards the warehouse.

There was only one girl who would fit that brides-maid's dress and that girl was Kate Lovat. So he had bet-ter gird himself to do some serious grovelling.

Attached to the wall was a modern nameplate with the words *Katherine Lovat Designs* in an elegant font.

It was classy but not stuffy or imposing. And it stopped Heath in his tracks.

Perhaps it'd been a mistake to underestimate Kate Lovat?

Kate had been an astonishing delight until he had opened his big mouth and put his foot in it. Surprising and intriguing and more than just attractive. She had a certain unique quality about her that Heath could not put his finger on and he was kicking himself for overreacting.

The breeze picked up some dry leaves and tossed them up towards Heath, bringing him back down to earth with a thump. He had to work fast. His father was already at Jardine Manor with Alice preparing the house for their wedding, which his son was organising so very brilliantly.

Heath slid his sunglasses into his hair and his smart black designer boots clattered up the well-worn stone stairs that led to the first floor.

He stretched out to press the doorbell just as he noticed that a piece of pink fluorescent paper had been taped onto the metal door. Someone had written in large letters:

*Casting today 10 a.m. to 2 p.m. Gents to the left. Ladies to the right. All leotards and tutus must be collected before you leave. Any lingerie left behind will be recycled.*

*Tutus? Casting?* Heath quickly checked his watch. Nine-thirty.

Amber had told him that Kate specialized in tailoring for women, but nothing about running dance shows! Surely designers used agencies for that sort of thing? Perhaps he had come to the wrong address?

The door was slightly ajar and, with a small tap on the frame, Heath opened the door and slipped inside the most remarkable room he had ever been in.

The entire floor of the warehouse was one single space. Large, heavy pillars supported the ceiling and no doubt the floor above. A row of tall sash windows ran the entire length of both sides of the room. Light flooded in and reflected back from the cream-painted brick walls, creating an airy light space with the quality of light he had only ever seen in an art gallery before.

He took a step further inside the room, the sound of his hard heels beating out a tune on the hardwood floorboards and echoing across the space. On each side of the door were changing areas made from what looked like tents hanging from the ceiling, and in front of the window was a very professional photo set-up with camera and lighting stands and lighting umbrellas and plain backdrops.

Someone had paid for the extras with this set-up.

But who? And where were they?

He strolled forward down the length of the room between two long white polymer worktables and a collection of ironing boards, tailors' models in various sizes, naked and partly dressed, and two draftsman desks covered with stacks of coloured paper.

Everywhere he looked were abandoned rolls of fabric, sewing machines and what looked like cutlery trays stuffed with scissors and all kinds of boxes and packets.

*So, all in all—his worst nightmare. Clutter and chaos. No sense of order or control. If he ran his office like this they would be out of business in a month.*

Blowing out hard, Heath shook his head and peeked behind an elaborate Japanese lacquered folding screen. And froze for a few seconds, scarcely believing what he was looking at before breaking out into a wide smile. It was the first time that he had smiled that day—but he had good reason.

Kate was sitting at a desk under the window, nodding her head from side to side as she sang along to a pop song in a very sweet voice.

Of course he could have interrupted her—but this was a totally self-indulgent pleasure he wanted to stretch out for as long as he could.

She was wearing a tiny lime-green strappy top, which was almost covered by a necklace which seemed to be made up of bright green and yellow baubles. Her short brown hair was tousled into rough curls with some kind of hair product that made it stand out from her head and yet still seem soft and appealing. *Touchable.*

As a tribute to the warm July sunshine which was streaming in from the window only a few yards away, she had chosen what looked like a tight stretchy tube to wear as a skirt, which covered her hips and upper legs but moved when she stretched across the table, revealing shapely tanned legs which ended in brown platform sandals. And those amazing painted toenails which had rendered him speechless the evening before.

It was strange how this colourful and totally unlikely ensemble only seemed to make her lovely figure even more attractive.

This version of Kate was startling. Entrancing, fresh and natural.

The elegant woman in the slick city suit, designer boots and smart make-up he had met the previous evening was gone, replaced by a slim girl in working clothes doing her admin early on a Tuesday morning. She did not need make-up or expensive clothing or accessories to look stunning—she was lovely just as she was.

The city girl in the suit he had met last night he could

deal with, but this version of Kate Lovat with the tape measure around her neck was far more of a challenge.

Was this her workshop? Or was she an employee of some bigger company?

He should have asked Amber a lot more questions before he'd left the hotel—background information was always useful for negotiations, and suddenly he felt out of place. This was Amber and Kate's territory, not his. This pretty girl who looked absurdly cute might not be so generous when she remembered how he'd slighted her the night before.

Either way, he was standing here in a black business suit and crisp white shirt on a summer day, feeling completely overdressed, while she was comfortable and cool in her work clothes. He had rarely felt so out of his depth, or so attracted to a girl who was totally natural and comfortable in her own skin. And what skin!

That kind of combination would spell trouble if he stayed around long enough to get to know her better. She was dynamite with a slow-burning fuse. And the last thing he needed was another complication like Olivia to deal with.

Her right hand was tapping with a pencil on a pad of drawing paper while her left was holding up what looked to Heath like an invoice or delivery note. She was peering at it through pink-tinted spectacles with bright-red frames then scribbling something down on the pad. Then looking back at the printed sheet, and then back to the pad. And scowling.

'Why is this not adding up?' she asked with a long

sigh, then reached out and rummaged through a large cardboard box which was overflowing with paperwork and ring binders and envelopes, pulling out individual sheets and tossing them onto the desk as she went until her fingers froze on what looked like a purple sticky note pushed inside an envelope. 'There you are,' she smiled, 'I knew that I had already paid you last week. Now stop hiding from me or I will never work out how to do these accounts properly.'

A self-satisfied smile flashed across her lips, which was so natural and unpractised that it made his heart melt just looking at her.

She looked so vulnerable and naïve.

And, judging by the accumulation of papers on her table, not the world's best bookkeeper. Her filing system could certainly use an overhaul and a simple spreadsheet would do all of the adding up she was struggling with. He could probably set it up in less than an hour, but somehow he didn't think that Kate would welcome another criticism of her working practices.

Not after yesterday. And certainly not from him.

Even if some part of him did yearn to dive in and sort out the mess she had clearly got herself into.

Heath was still working on some way of introducing himself without looking like a complete idiot when a voice behind him whispered, 'Hello, handsome. You're a little early for the casting, but if you want to take your clothes off over there, I'll be happy to take a look at what you can do.'

Heath spun around to find a tall, dark-skinned man

in a slim-fit red-and-green windowpane check suit and narrow Italian shoes scanning his body from head to toe while tapping his chin with a forefinger.

'I have to break the bad news to you, handsome. You don't look like a dancer from here.'

*Dancer? Remove his clothing?*

A woman's voice laughed out loud and he glanced over his shoulder to see Kate grinning from ear to ear. She exchanged kisses on both cheeks with the man and wrapped one arm around his waist. 'Lovely to see you, as always, Leo. And as punctual as ever. As for our guest,' she said in a semi-serious voice, 'I can see what you mean. Not really the dancing physique at all. Good thing he's my client and not looking for stage work.'

'Your client? Oh, I see. Pity. *Ciao bella.*' Leo coughed and strolled away towards the entrance.

'Good morning, Kate,' Heath replied calmly, trying not to squirm in the suddenly overwhelming heat. 'I'm sorry to disturb your work but I was hoping that you could spare me a few minutes.'

She looked up at him wide-eyed, then turned away and rested her hand against the wide table. 'Why? Are you interested in being measured for a suit?' She gestured over his shoulder. 'I specialise in ladies' wear but, as you can see, I have a wide selection of fabric in an assortment of colours. I'm sure I could find something to match your complexion. A fetching shade of puce embarrassment tweed, perhaps?'

And then she looked up at him through her eyelashes

and their eyes met. And in that instant he knew that she was already two steps ahead of him.

Kate knew precisely why he was there and had absolutely no intention of letting him get away with anything.

She ignored the stack of papers on her desk and started pinning pieces of thin tissue paper to a tailor's model, smoothing each piece in turn to fit the curves of the shape below. Her fingertips moved in slow languorous strokes, sensually caressing each piece, one after another, with infinite care and such loving attention that Heath's blood pounded just a little hotter.

He paused and tapped his head with his forefinger. 'Touché. Actually, I have come to apologise for yesterday. Then I'm going to thank you nicely for making four charming bridesmaids' dresses at very short notice to help me out. Is that better?'

Kate twitched her lips but turned back to her model and kept on pinning and smoothing until the entire bodice was covered with what looked like a jacket. Only when she had arranged the pattern pieces to her satisfaction did she whirl around towards him with her back against the desk.

Heath inhaled slowly and braced himself for whatever was coming his way. Which was why when she did speak what she said knocked him more than he could have imagined.

'I am curious about one thing. Did you come to me as the last resort? Because you left it too late to ask anyone else to make the bridesmaids' dresses?'

He winced and gave her a brief nod. There was no point

in denying it. 'Partly that,' he admitted. 'My father only announced that he was getting married a month ago. I had no idea that fashion houses need such a long lead time.'

And then he took a breath. 'But I also relied on Amber's judgement. She knows how important this wedding is, and would never have suggested Katherine Lovat Designs unless she was confident that you would do a good job.'

Kate sighed out loud through her nose and crossed her arms. She shook her head and clenched her small fingers into fists for a few seconds. 'And to think that I actually came all the way to your office yesterday, in the rain, to thank you for choosing me in preference to some big name couture fashion house.' Her knuckles wrapped on her forehead. 'Idiot.' Then she sniffed and started to stack the pile of papers on the table. 'Did you seriously hate the dress I showed you?'

'On the contrary. The colour is perfect for me but I suspect it would be a little snug across the chest.'

Her lips pressed together and she blinked several times but refused to look at him. 'Really? And what about the pearl embroidery on the bodice? All that embellishment that you have a deep aversion to.'

He took a step closer. 'It's lovely. Really lovely. Was it done by hand?'

Her head shot up and she stuck her neck out, open-mouthed. 'No, the magic elves came in the night. Of course it was done by hand.' She lifted both hands and waved them at him. 'These hands, to be precise.'

He tried to take that information in, but words refused to form.

'You did all of that pearly embroidery?'

She nodded slowly up and down. Once.

'For all four dresses? On your own?'

Kate replied with a small shoulder shrug. 'This is a one-woman show. No assistants, no apprentices. And I had to get the pearls just right. Otherwise the design wouldn't match the pearl embroidery on Alice's wedding dress.'

Suddenly she winced in pain as though she had cut herself and launched herself at him and grabbed the sleeves of his suit jacket. 'Oh, no! Look what you made me do. I should not have said that. Should. Not. The wedding dress has to stay top secret until the big day. You have to promise not to say a word to your father. Seriously. Not a word. Okay. Promise?'

'What wedding dress is that? Never heard a thing. Was someone talking?' he replied in a calm voice and pretended to look around the room for a few seconds before gazing into her green eyes, which were sparkling with passion and sunlight. 'But why didn't you explain that last night?'

'Because you were far more interested in your phone call than listening to anything that I would have to say.'

Kate released her grip on his sleeve and smoothed down the fabric before looking up into his face with an expression which demanded his attention and held it there.

'Why weren't you listening? Was your pride hurt because I actually used my initiative and did not follow your specific instructions to the letter?'

*Oh, Kate. If you only knew the kind of day I had yesterday you would understand why the dress was the last straw that burst the bubble of control I was clinging onto so badly.*

Her gaze stayed locked on his, but as he stayed silent she slowly relaxed her grip and a frown creased her forehead. 'So, it had nothing to do with me. Did something happen yesterday? Before we met? Something which rattled you?' she asked in a low intense voice which seemed to echo around the space even though they were so close that he could feel her breath on his throat and see the way the sun brought out the highlights in her hair.

It was as though she had read his mind. *Intuitive.*

'Rattled? I don't get rattled,' he mocked.

'Yes, you do,' she whispered and shuffled back half a step so that she could look up into his face. 'Talk to me, Heath. Tell me what rattled you so very badly.'

He looked into those green eyes and knew instantly that she was not judging him or condemning him—she simply wanted to know what had happened. But there was something else in that gaze. Not pity. Concern. She was concerned about him.

And it shocked him to the core that he could not recall a single time that a girl had looked at him with concern in her eyes and meant it. Not Olivia. Their relationship had been based on mutual convenience and shared interests and a healthy appreciation of the benefits of an active social and sex life. But not concern. Not intimacy. Not sharing their hopes and fears.

The silence lengthened and she did not try to fill the silence with chatter but waited patiently to hear his response. Her light floral perfume and the sheer physical presence of this tiny woman who was within touching distance combined with the intensity of that one single look to reach inside him and knock on the locked door of his heart.

And for the first time in years he knew that he could trust another person with the truth. The real truth.

'A few minutes before you arrived, my girlfriend, Olivia, called from China to inform me that not only is she going to miss the wedding this weekend, but she had decided that our relationship is not working for her and it was time to go our separate ways.'

'She broke up with you? Over the phone?' Kate's jaw dropped in disbelief.

'Over the phone from China. So you see, as of yesterday I am officially single and without a wedding date.'

'Oh.' She sighed and blinked several times. 'Well, to use my good friend Amber's favourite expression—that sucks. Big time.'

Heath exhaled the breath he had not even realised he had been holding in and his shoulders seemed to drop several inches. 'It certainly does. And that is not the only problem. Alice had insisted that Olivia should be one of the four bridesmaids. And now she isn't coming.'

Kate's eyebrows went north and her mouth formed a perfect oval. 'Ouch. Does Alice know yet? It could be difficult to find another bridesmaid in less than a week.'

'Tell me about it. You already know that Olivia is petite and has tiny feet—you made her dress. There aren't many girls who would be able to fit into...' His voice faded away as his gaze scanned Kate from head to toe and back again. 'Miss Lovat, I have a question for you.'

Her chin lifted. 'Hello. Yes? What is it?'

'What shoe size do you wear?'

'It depends on the shoe but usually a size three or four British sizing. But why do you want to know that? Because Amber has told me all about your deep-seated dislike of anything that comes under the category of female fripperies. So if you are thinking of buying me footwear for some reason, thank you, but no.'

'Me? Ah. No. Not my thing. Now, Alice...' he sucked in a breath through his teeth like a whistle '...Alice insisted on buying all of the bridesmaids' shoes from some exclusive London designer. I know this because I paid the invoice. And guess what size Olivia takes? A three. How about that for a coincidence?'

He sighed out loud and crossed his arms, lips pressed firmly together. 'Shame that I shall have to return those gorgeous shoes now that Olivia cannot make it. And I know how much Alice wanted to have four bridesmaids. Not five or three. It had to be four. This is going to be such a blow. I'm worried that it might even ruin her big day.'

He cupped one elbow and started tapping on his lower lip.

'Of course, there is one other alternative,' he said in a lilting voice. *While staring directly into Kate's eyes.*

'Any idea where I might be able to find a replacement bridesmaid at short notice who would fit a slim petite dress and size three shoes? Um...?'

# FOUR

_____

KATE STARED AT HIM, open-mouthed, for all of two seconds before she got the message.

'Oh no, you don't. Not a chance, Sheridan,' Kate replied with a short sharp laugh and stepped back, both of her hands palm upwards.

'You would make a perfect bridesmaid, Kate,' he grinned, 'and I'm sure Alice would be delighted.'

'Are you mad?' She glared at him in disbelief. 'I might have spoken to Alice on the phone and by email but I have never even met your future stepmother in person and you may not be aware of this but usually the bride likes to have some say in who her bridesmaids are, not the best man. She is bound to have lovely friends and relatives who were furious to be missed the first time around. Or ring someone in your little black book.'

'No point—the dress has been made for Olivia—and is about your size. In fact, didn't Amber say that you modelled it because Olivia was overseas?'

Heath stepped back and then walked in a slow circle

as he scanned her so slowly from shoes to head that she started to squirm. 'Although it might be a bit tight around the bodice, the length would work.'

Kate's head slowly came up and she crossed her arms over her chest.

'Ah, so that is the only selection criteria. I have to be short and flat-chested.'

'And pretty.' He shrugged.

'Short, flat-chested and with small feet,' came her choked reply. 'And not likely to crack the camera lens. My, you have a wonderful way of charming the ladies with your pick-up lines, Heath Sheridan. How could I possibly refuse when you hit me with that kind of flattery?'

Kate pressed her fingertip to her lips and laughed. 'Oh, wait. I do refuse. Sorry, Heath. Not this time, not any time. Not a chance. But don't panic. Alice is bound to know someone who would fit that dress.'

Heath crossed his arms and shook his head slowly from side to side. 'I researched every lady on the guest list last evening and not one of them is a match.'

'You have dossiers on the guests?'

'Of course. How else would I know how to engage the house party in idle conversation?'

Kate closed her mouth, inhaled deeply, lifted her chin, slipped the pin cushion back onto her wrist and gave Heath a finger wave. 'Well, I think that just about says it all. Best of luck with the bride. Have a lovely wedding.'

'Kate. Wait. You know I wouldn't ask you to do this unless I was desperate.'

'Yes, I am beginning to understand that very well.'

'Wait. This is important. I need this wedding to be a success,' he blurted out as she turned away from him.

And he just stopped himself in time before the words came tumbling out of his heart—but he pulled back.

*This might be the only chance—the last chance—that I have to build bridges and get my father back into my life.*

His true feelings were too personal and private to share with anyone. When it came to his parents, he was a closed book to the rest of the world and that was exactly how he intended to stay.

Kate lifted her chin and stood rock-still, her lips pressed together. Then she squinted at him and asked in a stubborn voice, 'Just give me one good reason why I should step in for your former girlfriend and be a bridesmaid when I haven't even met the bride and groom.'

Yes! A window of opportunity. And if there was one thing that Heath had picked up in ten years in publishing, it was that he had to make the most of each and every opportunity that came his way.

But what? What could he come up with? A reason?

His gaze dropped to the paperwork under her splayed-out fingers. The very messy paperwork which she was having trouble getting to add up. Which was hardly surprising if she was using sticky notes as receipts.

Yes. A bribe might just work.

'One?' Heath replied. 'I can give you several. But how about this for an idea?'

Heath took three steps towards Kate so that he was almost touching her and looked down into her startled face. 'I am prepared to offer you a trade, Miss Lovat. As a lady entrepreneur, you must be so incredibly busy with your creative designs that I suspect you could use some professional help to sort out all those pesky accounts and the mountain of business paperwork that comes with working for yourself.'

He stepped to one side, looked hard at the desk, then back into her face, and then back at the desk again.

He sniffed and waved one hand in the air. 'It just so happens that I am rather an expert in that particular area. I designed the office management system and helped to roll it out across the whole division. From what I have seen, I doubt that a company executive such as yourself would need more than a day or two to clear your backlog, bring your accounts up to date and put an easy but efficient system in place which could cope with any and all expansion plans. All I would need is some desk space right here in the studio. One business person to another. What do you say to that?'

He pressed the fingertips of both hands onto the surface of the table, trapping her within the arch of his body. And, to her credit, Kate did not shuffle away but locked her lovely green eyes onto his and refused to move. Only the longer he looked the more he wanted to look and it was an effort to blink, step back and focus on something other than her flawless skin and the amber and gold highlights mixed into the green of those eyes, which seemed to pop against the longest dark brown eyelashes that he had ever seen—and hers were real.

'Well, there you have it, Kate.' He laughed. 'One good reason why you should run away with me this weekend and be treated to full-on pampering—and all in exchange for wearing one of your lovely frocks. Say yes,' he murmured with his best molten-chocolate seductive voice. 'You know you want to.'

Kate inhaled deeply then blew out and wafted her hand in front of her face.

'Wow!' She laughed and waggled her fingers at him. 'Back off. Give a girl a minute here. I need some air if I'm going to think about it.'

Kate sat down heavily in her chair and dropped her head into her hands.

*Decision time.*

She could go back to her house and work on with some inventive ways to pay the rent and pretend that she did not care that Heath was one bridesmaid short of a wedding. A wedding which might direct a lot of high-spending customers to Katherine Lovat Designs. She had even printed off some extra business cards.

Or. And she closed her eyes for a second and inhaled a breath of hot dusty air.

Or she could agree to go with Heath to his father's wedding, put on Olivia's bridesmaid dress, which she already knew was a perfect fit, and new shoes and walk down the aisle behind a bride she had never even met.

In front of Heath's fancy Boston family and friends.

She glanced up at Heath, who had taken out his smartphone and was already scanning his messages as he paced up and down her workspace.

*Oh, Heath Sheridan. He is your dad and you love him and want him to love you!*

*If you only knew how similar we are, Heath. And how very different.*

Taking a deep breath, Kate sat back in her pedestal chair and scrubbed at her temples with the fingertips of both hands. But when she opened her eyes the first thing she saw was the overflowing box of invoices and receipts which had built up over the past few weeks—okay, months—which she had promised Saskia that she would sort out the minute the bridesmaids' dresses were finished.

No excuses. She had to face them. This was supposed to be her business and there was no way that she could afford an accountant, so it was her or relying on Saskia again. If only she knew...a business professional who might be willing to do her accounts for her.

Heath's voice echoed across from the other side of the work table. She caught the words 'margins' and 'discounts' before he turned away.

Kate got to her feet and started pacing up and down in front of her desk, glancing at the paperwork piled inches high around the boxes and then looking up at Heath.

Her steps slowed then speeded up again. Heath was a brilliant businessman—who was desperate for a replacement bridesmaid.

She was a hopeless businesswoman who was fairly desperate with her accounts.

Just looking at the boxes made her want to shove the

whole lot back into the cupboard to join the others and get on with the exciting work on Leo's ballet costumes.

This could be the chance that she had been looking for to finally prove to her parents that she was able to make a living doing what she loved and she was not wasting her life on foolish nonsense. Taking her income to the next level would certainly come in useful too.

But a weekend wedding with the Sheridans? Ouchy ouch ouch.

It took five circuits before she stopped and braced her legs.

*It might just work.*

'Hey, handsome. Over here. I've had a thought.'

'Shall I alert the media?' he snorted and immediately coughed into his hand as she glared at him. 'Sorry. Carry on. You've had a thought. Does that mean yes?'

'Not so fast. I need to get a few things straight.' Kate's breath caught in her throat and she carried on pacing slowly up and down so that when she replied her words came out in one long stream.

'I would just be there as a stand-in bridesmaid, right? Not a wedding date. You'll fess up that Olivia is not simply delayed somewhere.'

'Absolutely,' Heath replied, the ice in his voice replaced by a warm edge and there was just the touch of a smile on his lips. 'And I promise that the speeches will be short and the champagne chilled.'

Kate relaxed her shoulders. She had done it now. Might as well go the full distance. 'How about dancing and frolics?' she asked.

Heath stopped frowning and his eyebrows lifted. 'As far as I know, there are no plans for dancing. Or frolics. This is my dad, remember. But Alice has friends in a symphony orchestra who are sending up some of the string section. It should be a very cultural event. And why are you groaning again?'

'Promise me that you will never move into sales because you are doing a terrible job at selling this to me, Heath Sheridan.' Kate jutted her chin out. 'A cultural event? This is a wedding. You know, romance, fun, happiness.'

Then she sniffed and gave a small shoulder shrug. 'Is it a church or civil service or both?'

'The local village church.'

Kate nodded slowly. 'Let me guess. The Jardines have lived in the village for generations and have their own pew in the ancient church and plaques on the wall. Am I right?'

'How did you know that?' he asked in a low voice. 'Do you know the village?'

'No. But I have been to a few like it. English tradition.' Her gaze locked onto his totally confused and bemused face and she burst out laughing. 'You really do not have a clue, do you? Oh dear.'

Heath replied by stepping closer so that their bodies were almost touching. She could practically hear his heart beating under the fine weave luxury cotton shirt. But for once she held her ground and looked up into his face rather than give way.

'Let me check that I understand the deal,' she whispered. 'One all expenses paid wedding, complete with bridesmaid duties, in exchange for two full days of your time as a business consultant. And you would be doing the actual number-crunching—not some minion. Okay?'

Heath took her hand and pressed his long slender fingers around hers and held them tight just long enough for her to inhale his intoxicating scent. Combined with the texture of his smooth skin against hers as he slowly raised her hand to his lips and kissed the back of her knuckles, sensible thought became a tad difficult for a few seconds.

Because the moment his lips touched her skin she was seventeen again and right back on her doorstep.

'Better than okay. It's a deal. Delighted to have you on my team—because I don't have minions,' he replied with a full-on, headlight-bright grin.

'Team,' she whimpered. 'Right. Now that is settled. What time do you need me to be there on Saturday?'

'Oh, didn't I tell you? I'm going to need you there on Friday morning so you're ready for the wedding rehearsal and dinner. I hope that isn't a problem.'

'Think musketeers. Think swagger and swords. Think Johnny Depp.' Saskia Elwood picked up a cake fork and pretended to have a mock sword fight with the china teapot on Kate's kitchen table.

'Okay, okay, I am thinking and drawing at the same time. Designing pirate gauntlets is not easy, you know.'

'Never said it was—that was why I came to the best. You are the only girl I know who spends most of her life in a fantasy world inside her head. You are a saviour, Kate Lovat.'

'*Flatterer.* You know my hidden weakness for panto-mime,' Kate replied with a short salute. Then she looked at Saskia over the top of her spectacles. 'Why are you the person who always ends up running these projects when you have a business to run?'

Saskia shrugged then chuckled. 'I seem to have one of those faces that scream out—come and ask me to help and I will drop everything and do it for you. You would have thought that I would know by now, wouldn't you?'

'No—' Kate laughed and patted Saskia on the arm '—you have always been generous with your time and your heart. That's who you are. And I wouldn't want you to change a bit.' Then she gasped. 'Wait. I have had a bril-liant idea. Why don't you go to this wedding in my place? The dress might be a tad short but you've got the legs to get away with it. Heath wouldn't mind a bit.'

'What? And deny you the vision of Heath Sheridan standing in a sunlit old church in his grey morning dress? All tall, dark and handsome. Oh, I couldn't do that...not after your little teenage *interlude*.'

Kate rolled her eyes and sighed in exasperation. 'I should know better than to call you and Amber. Two hopeless romantics who are determined to overlook a few rather important facts about the brown-eyed heir to the Sheridan empire.'

She coughed and counted them out on her fingers. 'Let's start with the fact that he lives in New York and works in Boston. Not London. Boston. Then move swiftly on to the fact that he thinks I am a loon. And thirdly—and most importantly—the one and only reason that he asked me to this wedding is because I fit the dress I made for the girl who dumped him over the telephone. Do you remember the last boy you dated who was on the rebound?'

Saskia gave a dramatic shiver. 'Hugo the horrible stalker. How could I forget—but you seem to have missed something out.'

'His dress sense. All black single-breasted suits. Purrleese.'

'Actually, I was referring to the fact that he is both lustalicious and you like him. You like him a lot and you always have.'

'That's two things. I liked the old Heath who I met when I was seventeen and he was young and free and his mum was still around. That was eleven years ago, Saskia. We've both changed more than we could ever have imagined.'

'Um. Something tells me that he hasn't changed that much—he's still the same charmer underneath those executive suits.'

'I'm not so sure,' Kate sniffed. 'You heard what Amber said last night. Heath has been through an awful lot in the past ten years. First his mum's death, then his dad's love life, not to mention taking on a complete part of the family business on his own. That's a lot of weight for anyone to carry.'

'This is a wedding, Kate, not a business conference. You're going to have a great time.'

Kate opened her mouth, ready to agree with what Saskia had said, but all she could see in her head was that tension behind his smile. He was hiding something.

'Maybe. Maybe not. I'll let you know more on Monday.'

'Your studio. Ten a.m.—I'll bring the chocolate cake.'

'You're on.' Kate smiled. 'But I really should get ready, because it has to be almost ten by now.'

'Ten? Make that half ten.'

'What!' Kate replied and leapt to her feet. 'Why didn't you warn me? You know that my nana's old watch runs slow. And Heath is bound to be punctual. Oh, no! I need to do something with my hair. And shoes. I need shoes. Saskia!'

'Slow down. You're all packed and lovely. I checked your case and you have clean underwear and "kiss me until I die" shoes. All ready and waiting in the hallway. *You are going to have a fantastic time!* Now, you go upstairs and get sorted and I'll guard the...'

She hadn't even finished speaking when the front doorbell sounded and the clock in the hall chimed the half hour.

Kate didn't wait to reply and shot past Saskia, who was on her feet and strolling to the door. As Kate pulled on white capri trousers, a white and navy blue striped sailor top and navy lace-up shoes, she could hear Saskia chatting to someone and she peeked out of the corner of her bedroom curtains.

*Blood rushed to her head.*

A long slick black limousine was parked half on the pavement and half on the street in her narrow side road, which had been designed for the width of two horses pulling carriages.

She couldn't travel in a limo! And what would the neighbours think?

*Oh, no—too late.* The antique dealer who had the shop next door was already outside and peering into the shaded windows. Any minute now some uniformed chauffeur with a peaked cap was going to step out from the driver's side and wave a sub-machine gun around.

Well, good luck with that. Because his shop was full of tat and had one customer a week. If he was lucky.

Still. It was going to be weird having a new neighbour after twelve years.

And he did order six pairs of cream fine suede gloves every Christmas.

Kate sniffed. She hated change. It was so unsettling. Why couldn't things stay the same? Steady. Calm. After the chaos of her day job, it was actually quite nice to come home to her version of stability every night.

'Kate!' Saskia hissed from over her shoulder. 'Stop gawping out of the window and get yourself down here pronto. Otherwise Heath is going to be sitting in your parlour. There isn't room for a hunk that size in your kitchen and I can't leave him standing at the door much longer.'

'Don't you dare, Elwood!' Kate cried out and jumped off the bed. 'That parlour is my sacred space. No boys or any other type of person allowed.'

'Then move.' Saskia grinned, then started fanning herself with one hand. 'You're keeping the hot millionaire publisher and his limo waiting.' Her laugh escaped with a loud snort and she ducked and grabbed Kate's huge shoulder bag and took off down to the hallway.

'Oh, thanks. That is just what I need to put me at ease,' Kate huffed and tugged on a cut-off navy cotton jacket with gold buttons and epaulets. A navy and white silk scarf. Mother-of-pearl sarong clip to keep it all in place. One liberal spray of the old-fashioned floral vanilla fragrance that her grandmother had worn all of her life and she was good to go.

Kate took one final glance in the dressing table mirror and turned sideways before grinning at her reflection and winking.

She couldn't think about Amber's warning about Heath. She had to push down the flicker of apprehension and make the best of this wedding, one way or another, for the sake of her business.

Limos. Manor houses. Hot millionaires. Oh, yes! *Bring it on.*

# FIVE

HEATH KEPT LOSING his place in the financial report he had brought to read. Or maybe he was too distracted to make the effort to find it. Every time he started to work, he was interrupted by chatter, exclamations of excitement and questions from his travelling companion. But one thing had rapidly become only too clear.

*He had never met anyone like Kate Lovat.*

It was no doubt a lady's right to wear fragrance which filled the car with the smell of flower gardens in summer and not even the excellent air conditioning could cope with the way it seemed to linger on Kate's jacket and hair so that every time she moved a new waft came in his direction.

And she did move around. *A lot.*

Kate Lovat was an expert in the fine art of fidgeting. *The girl simply could not keep still.*

She had explored every inch of the car in intimate detail before they had negotiated the narrow street where she lived. The drinks cabinet and mini refrigerator had been particularly fascinating but she had soon moved on to the personal control settings and pressed every button and toggled every switch in the car like a toddler high on fizzy drinks packed full of sugar and artificial colours.

It was a new experience for him to meet a girl who had such an open and childlike enthusiasm for the new and was not afraid to express it.

The publishing professionals and booksellers he met in his work were focused on their careers and business plans. All working, heads down, all driven by a common passion for great books. *Eyes on the prize.*

Kate was like a squirrel. Leaping around on her seat as they passed one London landmark and then another, apparently only too happy to give him the complete tourist guide to the city he rarely visited these days and, when he did, it was only for business.

To Kate, London was a city of constant delight and amazement.

Heath tugged hard at the cuffs of his long-sleeved Sea Island cotton shirt, which had come from his favourite London tailor. His father had been the one who had decided almost a year earlier that he would open the London office and create a new marketing unit geared towards Europe and the Middle East.

Maybe it was simply coincidence that his father had started dating Alice Jardine again about a year ago?

Or maybe the London office was the excuse he needed to stay in England instead of working out of the Boston office where the company was based?

The team there rarely saw him these days and, for a private company in a challenging business environment, the one thing the employees needed was to see the company owner in his office or walking in the print room, talking to them and reassuring them that they had a future.

Not happenimg. Not yet at least.

But once this wedding was over...then they would have the talk.

*Once the wedding was over.*

Heath abandoned his report onto his seat table. Who was he kidding? It was never going to be over. Alice would be in Boston, living in the family house where he had grown up. And his dad would be even more distracted than ever, trying to keep his new bride happy.

The cellphone in the inside pocket of his suit jacket beeped discreetly and Heath glanced at the caller display before answering it.

'Good morning, Lucas,' he said, picking up the call and looking out of the window at the motorway verges. 'Or should that be good afternoon in Hong Kong?'

There was a guffaw down the phone from the jovial Canadian with a passion for books and selling them. 'Hot and humid afternoon. How about you? All gathered for the big wedding?'

'On my way now.' Heath smiled. 'So you would make my day if you told me that the meeting with the distributor went well yesterday.' There was just enough of a pause for Heath to take a breath. 'Talk to me, Lucas. What are the customers telling you?'

'It's the same story I had last week. Our competitors are stealing the market with enhanced digital versions of the printed academic textbooks. You know how students love visuals and they are so loaded up with technology these days.' Lucas sighed down the phone. 'I have been promising our customers some news on the new lines for over a year now, Heath, and your dad won't budge. I know this might not be the best time to bring it up again, but seeing as he is going to be in such a good mood...it has to be worth a try.'

Heath pinched the bridge of his nose between his thumb and forefinger. 'Leave it with me, Lucas,' he replied in a low voice, trying to conceal his disappointment. 'I'll do what I can.'

'Great, that's great, Heath,' Lucas replied a little too quickly and with enough tension in his voice to make Heath sit up a little straighter in his seat. 'But...there is something else you should know about. It's only a rumour, and you know what terrible gossips publishers are, but I heard it twice at the trade fair yesterday. You might want to check it out with the team.'

Heath ran his tongue over his suddenly parched lips. 'Oh, I think I have heard just about every possible gloom-and-doom scenario these past few months. What's the latest?'

'Only this. Sheridan Press is planning to move the printing operation overseas to cut down on production costs. It would be a shame—the Boston print works is a great selling point. But, hey—you know how rumours spread—there is probably nothing to it. I'll call you next week with the updates from the Beijing Book Fair. Have a great wedding!'

'Bye, Lucas. Thanks.' Heath snapped down the lid on his phone and held it in the palm of his hand.

*Move Sheridan Press.* This was the *last* thing that he wanted to happen.

And if the rumour was true? *If.* Then his father had kept his plans for the company a secret from the one person he had brought in to help turn it around. All the work that Heath had done with Lucas and their team had been geared to promoting books which would be printed by the loyal employees who had given Sheridan Press the best years of their lives.

Suddenly it felt as though the air conditioning had been switched to Arctic ice and a shiver ran across his shoulders. His shirt felt damp with cold sweat in the hollow of his back and his collar was trying to strangle him. Breaking the habit of a lifetime, Heath loosened the Windsor knot in his silk tie and unfastened the top button on his shirt, desperate to get some air into his lungs.

*Have a great wedding. Yeah. Right.*

Suddenly all of the missed phone calls and unanswered emails made sense. Charles Sheridan was well known for being low-key but Heath knew better than most that beneath that quiet, introspective grey-suited executive was a sharp and scheming brain.

*So much for working together.*

He had been a fool to allow ridiculous sentimentality back into his life. Memories of a happy childhood were just that—memories. For children who had no control over what happened to them.

*Stupid!* He had left his own company in the hands of the management team—and for what? To help out the man who had cheated on his wife with Alice Jardine and then married Julia Swan within twelve months of his wife's funeral? The man who had barely spoken to him in over a decade and then suddenly wanted to be reconciled and play dad?

Well, maybe his son and heir wasn't ready to be made a fool of.

The fire that had been burning inside Heath's belly turned into a furnace. Molten lava flowed through his veins and he felt his teeth grind together in frustration.

The surprises still kept coming, no matter how hard he fought to control his world.

His gaze fixed on a spot on the road ahead of them as the car took the motorway exit and stopped at a roundabout for a few minutes in the busy traffic before heading down a country road.

For one full second he thought about telling the driver that he had changed his mind and to take him straight back to the airport. And there would be a bonus if he broke the speed limit to get there. Why not? He had his luggage and passport. He could do what he wanted and go wherever he pleased.

But he wouldn't. And he couldn't. He had given a commitment to the printers who had made Sheridan Press one of the most respected names in the world. *And Heath always, always kept his word.*

*He could not go anywhere*—until he found out whether there was any truth behind this rumour or not. By talking to his father. Man to man.

It took a not so gentle pat on the arm to bring him back to the reality of a car on a road and the fact that he was not travelling alone—which was very unusual.

'Erm...Heath? I think your tie surrendered five minutes ago. It would be kinder to say goodbye and put it out of its misery rather than see it suffer any longer.'

*His tie? What?*

His gaze followed hers. Onto what had been a burgundy Italian silk tie from a top designer in Milan, which Olivia had given him as a Christmas present last year when they had first started dating and the chance of a real relationship seemed tantalisingly close.

Now his fingers were wrapped tightly around a screwed-up piece of rag which been twisted and torn until the life had been squeezed out of it.

His teeth clenched shut to suppress the expletive that was forming at the back of his throat. *Unbelievable!*

Kate put both fingers into her ears and hummed a pop tune. 'Can't hear a thing. Just get it out of your system. You'll feel much better.'

Heath looked at Kate, who had turned away and was still humming to herself, looked at the tie and then slowly, slowly exhaled the breath that he had not even realised he had been holding in.

Kate was looking out of the window with a beaming grin of childlike wonder on her face, transforming her from pretty into the kind of woman worthy of more than only a second look. Or even a third?

In her warehouse studio he had not missed the fact that Kate was the kind of pretty girl who looked good without make-up, but in the morning sunlight her skin appeared pale and translucent, in contrast to the bright sparkling green of those amazing eyes. But it was her smile, her bright-eyed, rosy-cheeked smile that hit him hard in the bottom of his stomach.

This version of Kate Lovat was a stunner.

Something twisted inside Heath's gut and he swallowed hard.

When was the last time he had taken the time to meet a woman outside the publishing world? A real woman like Kate? A woman whose life was as different as it could be from his relentless working hours and the endless battering of information and words.

He would give a lot to spend time getting to know this girl and find out what it was like to have one of those smiles aimed in his direction.

Except he did not have the time. He only had a few days before he needed to get back to Boston to carry out some serious damage limitation.

Olivia was right. His work had always been more important than their relationship. Strange. He had never been ready to acknowledge that fact before today and now it seemed to be staring him in the face.

He had spent the last ten years fighting each and every day to take control over his life in every way possible. His work. The people he worked with and even the women he dated. The way he lived and dressed—all tightly controlled.

Until he'd made the decision to move out of that life and try and reconnect with his father.

He chose to make that change.

His choice. His problem. And if his father was trying to use his sentimental need to be a son against him? He would deal with it.

So instead of punching the air or causing even more damage to his teeth by grinding them to powder in frustration, he slowly and carefully undid his tie, pulled it out from under the shirt collar and folded it into a neat coil on the leather seat.

Heath lifted his chin and was about to thank Kate when a crystal tumbler of sparkling liquid was thrust into his hand.

'Tonic water on the rocks. Enjoy.'

His first reaction was to pass it back with a cutting comment about how he would ask for a drink if he needed one. Except that his throat felt as though he had inhaled half of the Sahara desert. He did need a drink. Rather urgently.

'Thank you,' he whispered in a rasp and took one long slug and then another until the tumbler was drained.

'Excellent. Because I have made you another one. And you are most welcome. It is not every day that I get to play barmaid in a limo. I rather like it. Even if the entertainment is a little more action-packed than I would have liked,' Kate quipped with a casual tone.

'Entertainment?' he replied in a much better voice and

took a long sip of the cool drink and then another before turning slightly to look at her.

Kate was perched rather than sitting on the front edge of her seat, her hands folded neatly on top of a pad of drawing paper covered with markings. There was a pencil stuck behind her right ear and she was wearing spectacles. Rimless clear spectacles today, but spectacles all the same.

His gaze scanned her outfit, which he had been too distracted to notice properly before now. She was neat, beautifully groomed and as nicely dressed as any of Amber's friends. But different. Quirky. And there was definitely something in those eyes, which he suddenly realised were really quite a remarkable shade of green that told him that Amber's school friend was as observant and intelligent as any one of his team.

'Of course,' she replied. 'At least I found it entertaining.' Then her eyebrows lifted and she shook her head. 'I should make it clear that I don't usually listen to other people's telephone conversations but it is difficult not to eavesdrop when you are sitting a couple of inches away and bellowing about rumours about the company. I don't know what the rumours are all about—' she spread out one hand and waggled it from side to side '—but it sounded, well, dodgy to me.'

'Dodgy?' He choked on an ice chip and held up one hand when she moved forward to thump him. 'Not at all,' he coughed and spluttered. 'And I was not bellowing. I don't bellow. Bellowing is not my style.'

'How foolish of me. You were simply expressing your

excitement and enthusiasm for the topic,' Kate said with a smile but one side of her mouth was turned up. She had a dimple in her cheek.

He had never seen a dimple up close and personal before, but on Kate? Somehow it fitted her perfectly. How odd.

So she had picked up on the rumour angle.

He was going to have to watch what he said from now on.

A flash of light caught his eye and he turned back to the window but at that exact same moment he saw the reflection of Kate in the glass.

She was holding her spectacles in one hand while in one smooth movement her head dropped back, her eyes closed and her fingers combed through a head of boy-short conker-brown glossy layers with a gentle toss of her head.

It was the most sensual thing he had seen in a long time, and the fact that it was natural and completely relaxed made it even more remarkable.

The dark brown hair contrasted with Kate's smooth clear skin and, in the July sunlight streaming through the car window onto her slim frame, she looked about twelve. She had been at school with Amber, so she had to be late twenties. Maybe it was because she was so petite. Or should that be concentrated?

And it was definitely time to change to subject.

'What are you drawing?' he asked, and pointed to her sketch pad.

'Oh, nothing,' she said, 'just doodling,' and tried to flip

over the cover, but in an instant he had snatched the pad from her lap. She went for it but his long left arm held it high and firmly out of reach.

'Fine,' she sniffed and sat back in her seat with her arms crossed. 'Look at it if you want. I have nothing to hide. And no, I have not been taking notes about your so very important company information. Your trade secrets are safe with me.' And she gave him a quick salute.

Heath opened her pad and sat peering at the sketch for a few seconds before pointing to the page. 'What is it meant to be?'

'What do you mean?' she asked indignantly. 'What is it meant to be? They are gloves, of course. Gauntlets, to be precise. The local Christmas pantomime this year is Peter Pan and Saskia needs some swashbuckling specials for the auditions next month.'

'Pirates. Okay. And what about these?'

'Satin elbow-length prom-night specials. Very popular line. And not just white. Oh, no. The modern debutante likes violet and musk. I sell loads of those online.'

'Sell? Oh yes, of course. I hadn't realised that you made gloves as well. That must be a delightful hobby.'

*A hobby?*

Oh, Heath. Trust you to say precisely the wrong thing.

She could almost hear her father's dismissive voice. *'Oh, you'll soon get tired of that frivolous little hobby and start to do something serious with your life. But don't think we'll support you if you decide to throw your life away on worthless dreams.'*

*A hobby.* That was what they thought about her work. And now it looked as though Heath felt the same. Just when she was hoping that he was going to help her prove that her parents were wrong—by putting her business back on track.

Kate looked up into Heath's face as he flicked through the sketches she had slaved on for hours, evening after evening, day after day.

*And part of her died.*

He had no clue that his words had the power to cut her like a knife and leave her bleeding. How could he? He didn't know anything about her. All he saw was Amber's friend who sewed pieces of cloth into dresses and gloves. He probably didn't even remember coming to that high school party.

It would be so easy to pretend that the pages he was looking through so dismissively meant nothing and were only 'doodles'. That way he could go on believing that she was just another lowly dressmaker who was pretending to be a designer.

*But that was only a tiny part of who she was. And what she was capable of achieving—with or without his help.*

Kate dragged her gaze from Heath's long slender fingers as he stroked the pages and focused on the green fields and trees in the countryside at the side of the road. She pressed her lips together hard and swallowed down the burning sensation in her throat. She could use that cool drink she had just given away, but that would mean turning around and she wasn't ready to talk to Heath yet.

*What was she doing here? In this limo with this gorgeous man who didn't know anything about her world and her life?*

Kate pressed her right hand flat against her chest. Her heart was racing and she could feel the back of her neck burning scarlet as her mind raced.

Could she risk it?

Could she give him an insight into who she was and what she wanted in life? Show this man that she was her own woman with her own dreams and aspirations?

It would certainly make introductions to his family a little more interesting. And challenging.

Heath shuffled along the slippery leather seat next to her and she turned around inside her seat belt as he passed the sketchbook back to her with a nod. 'I'm afraid I am very traditional when it comes to gloves. Nothing like these.'

Kate stowed her precious sketches inside her tote. 'I will take that as a personal challenge. Leave it with me.'

Heath slid away but, before Kate could change her mind, she smiled across at him and added in a light voice, 'For once, Amber didn't give you an up-to-date resumé. I actually own a glove-making company in London. You have just been looking at some of my designs for next season's collection.'

He blinked. Twice. And she saw something new flash across his eyes.

Surprise. Astonishment. And intelligent awareness.

Almost as if he could hardly believe what he had just heard her say.

'You run two companies?' he asked and she heard just

enough incredulity in his voice to make her hackles rise and she lifted her chin as she fought back the reply she would like to give.

*Yes. Mr Smarty Pants publisher. I do run two companies. The small fact that I don't make enough money from both of them put together to pay the rent is neither here nor there.*

'Absolutely. I do have a day job in tailoring. But gloves are my passion. A girl can't have enough gloves.'

Heath's gaze scanned her face, his brown eyes slightly narrowed and blazing with intensity. The kind of intensity that warmed the already hot air between them on this sunny July day.

*Fool!* she told herself. *Now look what you have done.*

*You have just given Heath a peek inside your world and he doesn't know how to handle it. See. This is why you should have kept quiet. This is why telling other people your dream opens you up to feeling exposed and vulnerable.*

*Even if this person, this man, is the boy who you have lusted after for years. It still hurts when they cannot take you seriously.*

She mentally braced herself for the cutting remark or put-down.

It had happened so many times before. Like at the high school ten-year reunion that May where she had met up with Amber and Saskia for the first time in years. Those old classmates of hers had been scathing in their total contempt for her. *You? Running a fashion design business single-handed? Purrleese.*

Kate sat upright on the fine leather seat, waiting for

the put-down that would make it a lot easier for her to walk away in a few days.

'So, if I understand this correctly, you are running two different companies? Single-handed? Yes? That must make life complicated,' he said in a low voice.

Okay. So he was still reappraising her. She could deal with that in her usual fashion and laugh it off.

'Yes, I suppose it does. My choice. And they do say that variety is the spice of life. Don't you agree?'

Her heart rate increased to match the speed of her breathing.

*Say the right thing, Heath. Please don't make me hate you. Please.*

Heath replied with a smile that came from the heart and completely knocked her bravado out of the window.

'Not at all. I am singularly incapable of moving outside my area of expertise. Which makes your achievement even more impressive.'

He lifted his tumbler of melted ice and raised it in a toast. 'Congratulations, Kate. Running your own business takes a huge amount of work. Running two is extraordinary. All credit to you for taking that kind of risk. It seems that you have the better of me—I shall have to work extra-hard to keep my part of our deal.'

Then he shook his head before Kate could reply and chuckled. 'And now you have made me feel guilty about stealing you away from your work for a whole weekend.'

The tumbler slid back into its holder and Heath narrowed his eyes and tapped his finger against his full lips.

'This creates somewhat of a problem. How on earth am I going to make it up to you and give you a weekend to remember? Any suggestions?'

# SIX

___

KATE GENTLY PUSHED at the heavy oak door and poked her head around to see if this room was the library.

It was the fourth door that she had tried since leaving her palatial bedroom and en suite bathroom, which was bigger than her entire apartment and workshop combined. It had to be here somewhere and it certainly wasn't on the ground floor—they were huge public rooms intended for people who liked to live in style!

Thank heavens for the lovely housekeeper who had apologised many times that Alice and Charles could not be there in person to welcome her but they were delayed at the airport waiting for a flight. But she had strict instructions to show Miss Olivia Scott and Mr Heath Sheridan to their rooms the moment they arrived.

Kate had blustered out an explanation that she was here instead of Olivia but it had caused such confusion that after a few minutes she had given up and decided to go with the flow.

She stood on the wide wood-panelled gallery with the oil paintings of the Jardine family through the ages and glanced from side to side in the echoing silence of this ancient space.

The wide double doors at the end of the corridor with the ornate carving over the archway had to be the library.

She strode down the red handmade carpet and stretched out her hand to push open the door a little further. Then pulled it back again.

The knot which had formed in the pit of her stomach since those last few minutes in the car before they'd arrived ballooned into a football of tangled nerves and feelings and expectations.

That peculiar anxious feeling had taken root the moment Amber had asked her to make the bridesmaids' dresses for Heath in the first place.

And now she was actually here. At Jardine Manor! This was so surreal that she didn't know whether to laugh with happiness that she had pulled it off or cry because she knew that this could be the one single event that proved to her parents that she was not some pathetic joke and butt of all their jokes.

She had Heath to thank for all of that. So maybe, just maybe, she could lighten his load in some way and bring back his smile again while she was here? It was supposed to be a happy family occasion after all and who knew? With a bit of luck she might see a glimpse or two of the real Heath underneath his smart black suits?

Swallowing down her apprehension, Kate took a deep

breath, pushed her shoulders back, her chest out and her chin high.

*Time to get the Heath and Kate show on the road.*

The heavy door swung open with barely a creak and she strode inside.

Heath was sitting at a desk in front of a wide square window which flooded light into the dark wood-panelled library with its long floor-to-ceiling bookcases. Huge tomes, which had probably never been opened for years, filled the middle and upper shelves and, on the lower shelves, magazines and atlases and popular fiction.

All the books were behind glass to keep out the dust and she had to resist the urge to throw open every single one of those glass doors and let the air into the pages.

Didn't he know that paper and leather needed to breathe like humans?

But then, this wasn't his house. It was Alice Jardine's home and Heath would never do anything so impertinent as to try and rearrange her library.

'Ah. There you are,' she said with a smile. 'A girl can get lost in a place this big. Hello, handsome,' she said, trying to lighten his mood. He dragged his gaze from his laptop and turned towards her and his brown eyes locked onto hers and instantly the smile from his mouth reached those eyes and her heart leapt.

So what if she had to play the joker when he was around?

Every time she saw him, her reaction was exactly the same and the passage of time didn't seem to make a spot of difference.

*He was still the best-looking man she had ever met. And the only one who could make her toes curl up inside her shoes.*

And when he looked at her like he was now? As though he was actually pleased to see her? She was right back into crush mode. Heath Sheridan truly was the complete package.

She blinked a couple of times and covered up her embarrassment by peering at the books on the nearest shelf. She stepped back, waved her arms around and gave a half twirl. 'Have you seen this place? It's amazing.'

Heath crossed his arms and watched Kate skip up the circular staircase to peer at the leather-bound volumes which filled the lower levels of the heavy floor-to-ceiling bookcases.

'Cool.' Kate turned and looked at him over her shoulder. 'Would you mind if I brought a sleeping bag and moved in? I could have such fun here and you probably wouldn't notice in a house this big. Look at this library. I am drooling just at the sight of all of these books.'

She half twisted around towards him at the waist and pointed at her lower lip. 'See. Drool.'

He tutted. 'You look very fetching and there is no drool at all. Now please come down before you fall. Amber would never forgive me if you had an accident in those shoes.'

'This is true,' she replied, scrambling down from the step. She sat gracefully on the top rung, knees together, and tilted her head to one side before saying with a smile in her voice, 'You might have warned me that the Manor was actually a real, live Elizabethan manor house. I felt as though I should be paying an entrance fee for the guided tour. Does Alice actually live here? I didn't think people owned houses like this any more.'

'The Jardines bought the Manor several generations ago and yes, Alice definitely lives here.'

Heath paused then stood up and walked around the table so that he could look out at the garden and the gravel driveway beneath the library window. 'Speaking of which, I thought I heard a car pull up.' His voice dropped even lower and softer. 'And there is the lady herself.'

Kate strolled forward and stood shoulder to almost shoulder and followed his gaze. A tall man and a slim middle-aged woman were walking across the path from the flower beds towards the house. Her arm was around his waist and they were laughing and chatting away contentedly.

'Oh. Is that them?' Kate asked, peering over the stone window ledge. 'How sweet. They look like a lovely couple.'

The air between herself and Heath instantly dropped a few degrees in temperature and she could actually see his body bristle, his breathing fast and heavy.

'Yes, indeed they do,' he whispered in a low voice that was so laden with sadness and regret that she thumped his arm with the flat of her hand.

'Hey. Cheer up. They are family. This reminds me. Amber says hello. And when are you going to come out to India to spend time with her and Sam?'

'India?' he replied and turned back to his desk, her distraction technique a complete success. 'I might be able to get away early next year when I complete this current assignment.'

She nodded. 'Amber and I both know what that means. Next year, as in never.' Then she sniffed. 'She would love you to go out and ride elephants and eat coconuts and try out some of those academic skills on the girls. It would be great! Unless, of course...' she ducked down below his chin level '...you are sulking and feeling a teensy bit re-dundant. A girl still needs her big older ex-stepbrother now and then, you know. That never gets old.'

His eyebrows lifted and his shoulders moved into a small shrug. 'Is it that obvious?' he replied. And the hon-esty and openness of those few words tugged at her heart strings and pulled her in even closer.

Kate stood back to full height. 'Only to people who know you and who notice these sorts of things.'

'Well, that cuts down the options. She is happy. And nothing could please me more. It's just that I suppose I got used to sorting things out for her. And now she has Sam Richards to do that.'

'Well, that's nonsense. You'll still be her favourite stepbrother. But if you have any spare time, perhaps you could hire yourself out. Stepbrother for hire. One care-ful owner. Reasonable condition. Could last for years if fed and watered.'

'Think I would get many takers?' He smiled and her little heart lifted at the same time as the corners of his mouth.

'Absolutely. In fact, you'll be able to meet her real dad's

new family at Amber's wedding. All girls and all gorgeous. Won't that be fun?'

He snorted and started flicking through the papers on the table. 'I don't think that my idea of fun is quite the same as yours.'

'Fun? Now there's a thought. This house is gorgeous and perfect for a wedding, but so far I haven't heard any plans to have fun this weekend. Well, I am here and I am listening, so fire away. What does Heath Sheridan in his best man suit plan to do to kick off the proceedings with a bang?' Kate pressed the fingers of her right hand to the left side of her top, where she imagined her heart should be. 'And don't worry. Any naughty family secrets will be safe with me.'

Heath slumped back in his pedestal chair and whirled around to face her, open-mouthed.

'Naughty family secrets? Where did that come from?'

'Well,' Kate leant forward and fluttered her eyelashes at him, 'Amber did tell me about some off-the-wall expressionist paintings that you insisted on taking her to see at one time.'

'It was a passing phase. Like strawberries dipped in white chocolate. I moved on. Anything else?'

'Strawberries dipped in chocolate. Now you are talking my sort of language. That sounds delicious—and is now officially added to my must-try list. But you're avoiding the question. Out with it, Sheridan. What do you do for fun these days?'

'Sorry to disappoint you, Kate, but I spend most of my time chained to the computer. If I have a free weekend

I might take in a gallery or the occasional theatre or a local restaurant. That is my idea of fun. So can we move on now so I can get back to organising this wedding? The remaining guests will be here in a few hours.'

'Not a chance, Sheridan,' Kate hissed and slipped into the gap between Heath and the desk so that she was blocking his view of the screen.

'You still owe me a dance from a high school party. Remember that?'

His fingers stilled on the paperwork and he glanced sideways at her, his gaze burning into her face as though looking for something, but when he spoke his voice was gentle and there was a spark in his eyes which illuminated his whole face with an inner glow.

Kate inhaled sharply through her nose.

There he was.

There was the real Heath. Saskia had been right. There was the man who she had fallen in crush with. He was still there. And still capable of making her melt with one look.

*Heartbreaker Heath was back in town!*

She would have collapsed with relief if she wasn't already sitting down.

'High school? I'm surprised that you still remember that.'

*Remember? Forgetting was the problem.*

He was watching her now, waiting for an answer. But to tell him the truth would reveal how important that dance had been to her and that would be bad news for both of them.

'Of course. In fact, Saskia, Amber and I would be prepared to give you excellent references. This could come in handy if you should ever choose to change direction and go into the male escort business. Now, don't look at me like that. You never know.'

'I think I shall keep that one for a last resort.' He coughed, his neck a lovely shade of red.

With that, she slipped down from the desk and rearranged her top and jacket.

'Righty. Time to go and meet my hosts. I suppose I had better get my story straight before I march in to say hello. What, exactly, did you tell Alice about me when you broke the bad news about Olivia?'

Heath started fiddling with the power cable on his laptop. 'Sorry, what was that?'

*'Heath,'* she whispered with a questioning lilt at the end of the word, and stood directly in front of him and peered into his face.

'Oh, no. I don't believe it,' she gasped and slapped the table. 'I can see it in your face. You haven't told them, have you?' She flung her arm out towards the door. 'They are still expecting your Olivia to turn up. Aren't they? No wonder the housekeeper kept calling me the wrong name.'

She half closed her eyes, planted a fist on each hip and stuck her chin out at him.

'Heath Sheridan, I could strangle you. You have had three days to call, text, email, fax and maybe even send a carrier pigeon. But, no. And don't you dare say that it slipped your mind—because I saw those spreadsheets just now and every tiny detail of this wedding is right there in black and white. And sometimes highlighted in red.'

She was shouting now, totally in his space and almost touching and did not care.

Her finger prodded Heath twice in the chest. 'Talk to me, Sheridan. Because you had better have a very, very good reason why I shouldn't pack my bags and head back to London this very minute. Because I will. I mean it.'

'Oh, I'm so sorry to hear that, Olivia,' a sweet musical voice said from behind her shoulder and Kate whipped around to see the same smiling middle-aged woman she had spied outside, strolling across the library floor to meet them. 'I was so looking forward to finally getting to meet you. Heath, darling, won't you introduce us?'

Heath darling seemed to stretch his back several inches taller, his jaw made of ice and stone. 'Good morning, Alice. How nice to see you again. Of course. I am sorry to say that Olivia couldn't make it so my friend Katherine Lovat has agreed to take her place. I believe that you two have already spoken. Kate was responsible for those superb bridesmaid dresses.'

He glanced down at Kate with a look of pure steel. 'So, if you will excuse me, I will go and catch up with my father. We have a few last-minute business matters to clear up before the fun starts. I'm sure that you ladies have a lot to talk about.'

'Of course it was Charles's idea to have the wedding at the Manor. I'm afraid that I embarrassed myself by crying for at least an hour after he proposed. We have waited so long for this moment, but I didn't dare hope that we could make it happen. I had already refused him twice, but somehow I just knew. This was the right moment.'

'Charles proposed before? Oh, how romantic. I have to know—why did you turn him down? Cold feet?'

Alice smiled and shook her head. '*Cold son*. Charles tried to reconnect with Heath so many times over the years and I didn't want to come between them, even if it meant being apart. Did Heath mention that we're having a dinner party after the wedding rehearsal this afternoon? I do hope that it will help to break down any awkwardness.'

Kate finished off a mouthful of the most delicious chocolate cake before taking a sip of tea and shaking her head. 'Not a word. You see, this is what happens when you leave boys in charge. They don't pass on the essential details. As for the proposal? Crying for an hour is nothing. I would cry for a week! It sounds very romantic.'

Alice grinned and loaded up her plate with another slice of cake. 'You're very sweet. Charles says the same thing, but after the past few weeks? I can see now why other people pay wedding planners.' She licked the icing from her cake fork. 'I thought it would be simple to hold it here with just a few family members and friends to help celebrate, but I had no idea how complicated the whole thing could be.'

'*Complicated?*' Kate repeated and shuffled forward to top up the teacups.

Alice hummed slightly and popped a large piece of cake into her mouth.

Kate took the hint. 'Ah. Heath. I know, but he does care. Amber adores him, and I've known him for years. It just takes a while for him to get used to things. Everything will be fine, and I'm sure that he'll give you a marvellous welcome into the Sheridan family.'

Alice put down her cup and smiled at Kate, then brought her knees up and curled up on the sofa. 'Heath hates me,' she whispered, and gave a small shoulder shrug when Kate tried to deny it.

'There's a lot of history which he hasn't told you about. You see, Heath's mother, Lee, was a very good friend of mine. We were at high school together and then at art college in London. Lee was lovely,' Alice said with a really warm smile, 'and I couldn't want for a better friend. We made the effort and stayed in touch over the years. I used to go to Boston several times a year teaching art classes, and Lee used to come to London for girlie weekends. It was great and we had the best fun.'

The smile faded. 'It broke my heart when she was diagnosed with an inoperable brain tumour. We had so little time together at the end, so I put my life on hold and moved to Boston for a few weeks. Does that sound crazy to you?'

Kate reached out and took Alice's hand in hers. 'Not in the slightest. I have two wonderful friends, Amber and Saskia. I would do anything for them. Anything. I understand completely. I'm so sorry for your loss. I'm sure that she was grateful that you were there but it must have been horrific. That was so brave of you.'

Alice brushed a finger under her eye. 'I wanted to be

there for Lee, but for Charles and Heath too. Those last few weeks were an emotional turmoil for all of us and I was alone in the city and Charles was there and grieving and, well, when she died we comforted each other in the only way we knew.'

Her tongue moistened her lower lip and Alice reached out to the teacup in the silence that followed, but her hand was shaking too much to pick it up.

'I'm not proud of what happened. But it was totally right at the time. I had fallen in love with Charles Sheridan and I knew that he loved me, but the timing?' She rolled her eyes towards Kate and smiled. 'The timing stank. Don't misunderstand, Kate, we both knew that these things happen in times of crisis and trauma. People need comfort and support and sometimes words are not enough.' She looked down at her hands. 'We both agreed to step away and work out if these feelings were real or temporary before starting a long-term relationship so soon after Charles had lost his wife, who had been my friend. Our love didn't make me feel less guilty, and I know Charles felt that he was almost betraying her memory, but it was so hard to stay apart.'

'That must have been terrible for both of you,' Kate replied in a low voice, which was almost a whisper. 'Such conflicting emotions.'

Alice looked up at Kate and took her hand. 'It was terrible for all three of us. That's why I'm telling you all of this when we have only just met. Heath found us kissing one afternoon when he came home early from university.' She closed her eyes. 'I thought things were difficult, but then it became impossible. Heath was traumatised and he has never forgiven his father, or me, for betraying his mother's memory.'

Kate blew out long and hard. 'Alice, that was years ago. He's a grown man now.'

'It doesn't make any difference. Some things don't go away and nothing we do seems to help the situation.'

She pursed her lips. 'First of all Charles invited him to come in and help with the company, father and son, turning around the business side by side. And then I thought that asking Heath to be the best man would help him come to terms with the fact that I am in his father's life, which means I'm in his life too. Neither of those things has worked out so well. Frankly, Kate, I don't know what else to do to bring them closer together and make a family again.'

A single tear ran down Alice's cheek and Kate immediately shuffled over and put her arm around the shoulder of this woman who she had only just met.

Alice shook her head. 'You see what he does to me? I blurt out my whole life story when I'm sure that you would much rather be enjoying yourself back in London. I am so sorry.'

Kate turned around and faced Alice, passed her a tissue and smiled up at her.

'Don't be. Heath doesn't hate you. The only reason that I'm here today, at this minute, but talking to you and making a new friend, is because Heath was worried that your wedding to his father would not be perfect unless you had four bridesmaids. Not three. Four. He cares about you and his father and the business. That's why he wanted to help with the organisation. But he doesn't know how to tell you how much he cares. So he brought me along in place of Olivia because he didn't want you to worry. And I am very glad to be here.'

Alice gave a thin but warm smile, reached around and hugged Kate. And it was the warmest and most loving hug that Kate had enjoyed in a long time.

'Me too,' she said and blinked several times.

'Now, that's much better.' Kate grinned. 'Because you seem to be forgetting one very important thing. You—' and she pointed at Alice '—are the star of the show and we all have to bow and scrape before your goddess-ship. Okay? Okay. You leave Heath to me and focus on having the best weekend of your life. You are getting married to the man you love and who loves you back. Isn't that fantastic?'

'Do you know what? It is fantastic! And I *am* going to have the best weekend of my life.'

'Absolutely, and now we have that out of the way, may I see your engagement ring?'

Alice hesitated then stretched out her left hand to Kate, who grasped her fingers and almost choked on her cake when she took a look at the enormous heart-shaped diamond set in white gold.

'Wow,' she said breathlessly. 'That. Is some rock. That man is giving you some serious love here.'

Alice blushed and gave a small giggle, which reminded Kate so much of Saskia as she looked up and smiled at this woman who was still capable of being turned into a girl by a piece of jewellery. Alice pulled back her hand and bashfully replied, 'You might well be right. And I'm so embarrassed.'

'Why? Love can hit you any time of your life, there's no need to be ashamed of that.'

'Didn't you notice?' Alice said. 'My fingernails have been chewed to the quick over these past two weeks, building up to the wedding. I don't want Charles to be ashamed of me in front of all his important guests and at the social functions we're going to be attending. What do you think of acrylic nails? I've never used them before but it might be the right time to try.'

Kate shook her head very slowly from side to side. 'Don't go there,' she said. 'Trust me.' And then she smiled. 'You look lovely, Alice, and the last thing Charles will be thinking about tomorrow are your nails. He'll just want you to be happy. Right?'

'Yes, of course. How foolish of me. I just want to make it perfect for him. Charles is taking a terrible risk marrying me and I want to be the best I can.'

'Now, that I understand perfectly.' Kate paused and looked down at Alice's hands. 'You take about a size seven and five-eighths in gloves, don't you?'

Alice blinked. 'Yes, I have big hands and feet.' Then she looked at Kate in confusion. 'Does that matter?'

'It matters to the gloves.' Then Kate shuffled forward. 'You need gloves, girl. Classy, elegant and formal or informal as you want, but you need gloves until your nails have grown back the way you want them.'

'That is a fantastic idea.' Alice blinked. 'I don't know

why I didn't think of that earlier. Of course, you are right. I love gloves.' And then she slumped. 'But where am I going to find gloves to fit my enormous paws in the next few hours?'

Kate grinned. 'You happen to be looking at the sole proprietor of Lovat Gloves of London. We specialise in making boutique gloves for private clients. I think I might be able to fit you in at short notice. What do you say? Lacy bracelet length? Or silk satin elbow? No, don't answer. I'll bring the lot.'

'Why, Katherine Lovat—' Alice smiled and lifted her teacup in a toast '—here's to you. You are certainly full of surprises. I shall expect you to dance at my wedding.'

Kate clinked her teacup very gently for fear of breaking the delicate porcelain. 'Alice, I fully intend to.'

Ten minutes later Kate stepped out of the front entrance and stood blinking in the warm July sunshine. She had only got lost twice this time. Heath had not gone back to the library and she scanned the grounds to see if she could track him down.

And immediately spotted him. Only this time he was not alone.

Heath was standing with a look on his face which matched the stone blocks in the old arbour, next to a tall man who looked so much like him that it was impossible to mistake. This had to be his father. And Lord, there must be a lot of tall genes in that bloodline because Charles Sheridan had to be at least six feet two inches in his shiny black lace-up shoes.

And Kate's heart sank. Every part of Heath's body was pointing forward, or to the side. Any direction away from his own dad. His gaze was locked onto his tablet computer and, as she watched, he passed it across to the older man, who was standing only inches away, their shoulders almost touching.

*In silence.*

Their jackets might almost be touching but the icy hostility was all there to see.

Not just the fact that they both thought it appropriate to wear suits with shirts and ties on what was forecast to be a warm, sunny July day. She could understand formality and their personal standards when it came to how to dress—she knew all about that.

No. It was because watching Heath and his father reminded her so much of the frosty relationship that she had with her father and mother that the sharp pain of unwelcome tears of regret and disappointment pricked the corners of her eyes.

She had tried so hard, time and time again, to help her parents to understand her passion for gloves and what they called the silly outfits that she made. Fashion shows, award ceremonies, even weddings. And it had all been in vain. They wouldn't change their minds.

It was almost as if she was watching her own failed relationship acted out in front of her on this sun-kissed lawn.

Neither of them willing to give way or compromise. Both of them stubborn and determined to win the argument—any argument.

*Oh, Heath! You were supposed to be working with your dad to celebrate his wedding—not battling with him.*

*But he might need a little nudge from her to help him along the way.*

Yes. She had promised Alice that this was going to be the best weekend of her life and Heath was not the only one around here who kept their promises.

She might have failed to win over her parents—but she could do something to help Heath.

Kate stepped back inside the hallway for a few seconds, desperately trying to think through some kind of plan, when a girl wearing a T-shirt with the name of a famous London catering company dodged past her carrying a stack of tablecloths. It was the same company that Saskia had used a couple of times. Maybe the chef was making a splendid cake that Heath could carry in on a silver tray?

*And drop it on his father's head.*

She whirled around and followed the girl through a set of highly decorated and clearly original wooden doors into the most stunning dining room.

Sunlight beamed in through a row of mullioned windows with small squares of glass, created in a time when glass was a luxury and hard to make. Larger panes had been painted with the coat of arms of the Jardine family. Glorious swirls and mythical creatures danced on a shield with proud swords and what looked like falcons.

The Jardines had certainly been flamboyant.

*Unlike this room.* Plain oak-timbered walls below a ceiling braced with heavy wooden beams broken only by the occasional carved boss. Polished oak floors and large sturdy tables and chairs.

No colour apart from a lot of brown.

Oh, dear. Not exactly a fun venue for a wedding rehearsal party.

*Unless, of course, someone did something to change that.*

It only took Kate a few minutes to confirm with the catering team that yes, this *was* where the rehearsal dinner party was going to be held, and no, as far as they knew, the only decorations were plain white table linens and some silver candelabras belonging to the house.

Kate strolled back into the hall and flipped open her cellphone. A plan was starting to form inside her brain and she had to rein it in before it ran away with her.

'Saskia, it's me. I'm here. And yes, it does look like something out of a Tudor history book. But that's not why I'm ringing. Do you remember all of those party decorations we got together for Amber's birthday in May? Yes? Do you still have them? You do? Excellent. Because I need to borrow everything you've got in time for a party this evening. Balloons too. Yes, I know it's cutting it fine.'

She quickly checked her watch and added ten minutes because it was always slow. 'I can be there in about two hours, if that's okay with you? Yeah. Great. Don't worry about the heavy lifting. I shall bring Heath with me. He needs some time out away from here. But I'll talk to you later. See you. Bye for now. And Saskia, get an invoice ready. Heath owes you. *Big time.*'

Kate looked up just as Heath took a step towards his father, his face rigid with tension and his right hand holding the blameless computer as though he was about to smash it into something hard. Like his dad's face.

*Intervention time.*

Kate lifted her chin and strode out of the entrance and onto the stone patio at the front of the house, squaring her shoulders and with her full-on charm offensive smile.

'Heath! There you are.'

The two men turned around to face her, and from the looks on their faces she wasn't entirely sure if they were shocked or pleased with any excuse for the interruption.

She zoned in on his father and stretched out her hand and grinned. 'Hello, you must be Charles. How lovely to meet you at long last. I'm Katherine Lovat, fashion designer to the stars, but do call me Kate. All of my friends do.'

To give him credit, Charles Sheridan recovered remarkably quickly and calmly accepted Kate's rather warm chocolate-cake sticky hand and, surprisingly, shook it with a genuine smile.

'Then it would be my pleasure to call you Kate. But only if you call me Charles.'

'Charles,' Kate repeated and cocked her head to one side. 'You don't look like a Charles to me, and I certainly don't think Charlie would be appropriate. Do you? No, I think that Chuck suits you much better. Much friendlier. Don't you agree, Chuck?'

There was a short cough from Heath but she smiled over her left shoulder at his stunned face for a flash of narrowed eyes before whirling around back to Chuck.

'Well, Kate, I haven't been called Chuck since I was at

college.' Then he shrugged and snorted out a laugh which was so like the one she had heard from Heath in the library that it was astonishing. 'Why not? They were good times and I happen to be getting married tomorrow. You may address me as Chuck as many times as you wish.' He blinked, looking rather startled at the words coming out of his mouth.

'Excellent,' Kate replied and looped her arm through the crook of his elbow. She looked dramatically around in all directions before leaning closer and whispering, 'Now, down to the important stuff. Has Heath told you about his plan for the party this evening?'

A look of absolute astonishment crossed the older man's face and he raised his eyebrows at Heath, who was staring at her in disbelief.

'Not exactly, no. What precisely did he have in mind?' Chuck asked in a voice filled with dread.

'Oh, you boys are always talking business. Time for a break. Heath didn't want to spoil the surprise but we are going to decorate the dining room with party paraphernalia guaranteed to bring a bit more fun into the proceedings. As Heath says, a girl deserves to be spoilt for one evening. But don't worry,' Kate gushed. 'It will all be in very good taste. I am thinking balloons and bunting and banners. All the other guests can have fun helping to put it up and decorate the room.'

Then she stopped talking and drew back. 'I do hope that's okay with you, but it's meant to be a surprise. So you shall have to distract Alice from going in until the very last minute. Do you think you can do that?'

To his credit, Chuck only paused for a moment before nodding. 'Of course. Alice is very busy with the wedding arrangements. Hence the outside catering this evening. I'm sure that won't be a problem.'

'Did you hear that, Heath? We are good to go.'

His reply was the slightest shake of his head and his jaw stiffened.

Kate glared at him but he was not giving her any help at all. So she turned her winning smile onto his father and slid her hand onto his arm again.

'Only one small problem. I have foolishly left some of the party things back in London and I don't have transport. Would you mind if I borrowed a car for the next few hours? I am a very careful driver and Heath will be coming along for the heavy lifting.'

Chuck smiled to himself then fished a set of car keys out of his trouser pocket. 'I would pay money to see that. Have fun, little lady.'

And with a final flourish he dropped the keys into Kate's palm and closed her fingers around them. 'It has been a pleasure to meet you, Kate. A real pleasure.'

'Likewise. See you later, Chuck. I'll save you a dance.'

Charles Sheridan the Third paused in his stride for just long enough to shake his head before strolling into the Manor.

Kate lifted up the keys to a four-by-four and dangled them towards Heath but never got the chance to speak before he grabbed her by the arm and half dragged her towards the ornate gardens and did not let her go until they were hidden from the house by a tall hedge.

'Hey! You have to stop dragging me behind the bushes. People will talk and I have my reputation to consider.'

Heath replied by glaring at her and raking both fingers back through his hair.

'Your what? Kate Lovat, you are the most exasperating and impulsive woman that I have ever met. You seem to spend most of your time living in some fantastic fantasy world. Then just when I need you to be sensible and not embarrass yourself and me, you do something off the wall like this. Please explain before my head explodes.'

'Calm down! For some odd reason I actually want you to have some kind of relationship with your parents. And yes, as far as I am concerned, Alice is your new parent whether you like it or not. And don't look at me like that.'

She stabbed herself several times in the chest with her forefinger. 'It may have escaped your notice but I am a girl. Girls need to feel special. Especially when they are about to get married. Now—' she nodded slowly '—I am confident that you have an excellent checklist all ready for the wedding rehearsal this afternoon. I am expecting floor plans and timings, and I can see from your blushes that I'm not going to be disappointed, but here is your chance to do something remarkable. Something above and beyond the call of duty. Because you are going to start the celebrations with a fabulous rehearsal dinner party this evening.'

She sniffed and brushed imaginary crumbs from her fingers. 'Heath the hero. Job done.'

Heath stood back up and looked in silence towards the silent house, where two of Alice's younger cousins had just arrived, before replying in a tone of total disbelief, 'So you expect me to organise a party? For this evening? Without any advance notice?' And he shook his head slowly from side to side.

Kate held out the side of her jacket and gave a small curtsey. 'You are welcome. Leave the extras to me. In return I shall expect you to willingly volunteer to stand on a ladder and attach a range of bunting and balloons to the ceiling. And smile while you are doing it. Right? Of course right. The other guests will be dragooned and shanghaied into similar duties and you will all have a thoroughly enjoyable time. Now,' she said, checking her watch, 'we don't have much time. I need to get back to my place to pick up some gloves and then to Saskia's for the party stuff, then whizz back here pronto to put it all up...and where are you going?'

'This was your crazy plan and I have a mountain of work to do.'

Kate grabbed hold of his hand and held it with all of the strength that she could muster.

'Not a chance, Mister. I wasn't kidding just now. I need someone who can do the heavy lifting and that person is you. Joining in and doing something different just to please your old pater. Making it convincing. Right?'

'You cannot be serious.'

'I have never been more serious in my life. But relax.' She laughed as he groaned. 'You can work in the car if you must. How bad can it be?'

# SEVEN

---

*HOW BAD COULD IT BE?*

Until that morning Heath had no idea how frustrating it was to be a passenger in a car, which smelt of his father, being driven by a girl who insisted on keeping below the speed limit on every single road, lane, highway and alley between the Manor and the quaint London street where she lived.

It had become very apparent, very quickly, that Kate had not owned a car since passing her driving test. Why should she when she lived in London and worked in London and enjoyed public transport in London?

So basically he was sitting next to a girl who had not driven a car for ten years. The concept of a global positioning system was a mystery to her and he had been obliged to use his smartphone to compensate for her total lack of a sense of direction after they had driven around the same roundabout three times looking for the exit back to London.

The real problem, of course, was that with the radio

on and Kate chattering about the party extras which she wanted to pick up from Saskia's house, his mind was running on overtime and top speed about the conversation that he had just had with his father back at the Manor.

Just when he thought that he was starting to create some form of working relationship with his father, Charles Sheridan had confirmed his worst suspicions.

*The rumours were true.*

He *had* been looking at contract printing overseas. No decisions, not yet, but to him it really was a viable option. Other companies and publishers were doing it, so why couldn't Sheridan Press?

But what really stung was that his father simply could not understand why Heath was so angry at not being informed when the market was already buzzing with rumours about the future of the Boston print works.

They had worked together for weeks on the new promotional campaign that Lucas was rolling out and not once, during all of those chatty business dinners and coffee breaks, had his father said one word about looking for other book printers.

Communication skills were clearly not a Sheridan strength.

Heath pressed his fingertips firmly into his forehead and tried to drill some insights and flashes of inspiration into his skull.

Perhaps he should be thanking Kate for providing him with a valid excuse to walk away from his father that morning and snatch the thinking time he desperately needed on his own.

The ramifications and pressure of what he needed to do and how fast he needed to work burned through his mind, so that by the time Kate bump parked the truck of a car onto the pavement outside her house, his nerves were shot, he felt exhausted and his shoulders ached with tension.

It was with huge relief that Heath could finally stretch out his long legs and he ran around to her side of the vehicle to open the driver's door for her.

'How very gallant.' She smiled and grabbed her bag from the foot well of the car. 'I must say you have been an excellent passenger and not criticised my driving once, despite the small diversions now and again, and for that I thank you. In fact, you have been so splendid that if you want to come inside for a moment as a special treat I will let you peek inside my parlour.'

She turned on the pavement and leant closer towards him. 'I don't usually allow visitors to see where the magic happens, you understand, but in your case I'm prepared to make an exception.'

'How can I possibly refuse such an enticing invitation?' he said, smiling. Some of the exhaustion rolled off his shoulders as he waited for Kate to find her keys in the huge shoulder bag and open up the shop in the unbroken sunshine.

The quiet street was a mixture of private homes and small shops, no more than two storeys high. All of the buildings must have been homes at one time and some of them had been converted into shops at the bottom floor.

It was really an enchanting area. Quiet but close to the hustle and bustle of the city.

The sort of place where a person could get to know their neighbours in the community and make a home. He almost envied Kate for having that privilege.

The only place he had ever truly called home was the tall stone-built house in Boston, where he had lived with his parents until he was seventeen. Since then home had been university accommodation, followed by a series of hotels, apartments and rented houses like the one he was living in now. Efficient, modern, clean. But not home.

Strange. He had never really thought about that until today.

Tiredness did that to people. Made them melancholy. And he was tired, so very tired.

Maybe next week he should make the effort to take some time out and relax more. The next few weeks were going to be tough. He needed to stay sharp. Even the keenest knife needed to be sharpened now and again.

Suddenly there was a rustle of papers and movement and he looked around just as Kate beckoned to him to follow her into the hallway of her terraced house.

When he'd come around to pick her up that morning, Saskia had chatted away merrily to him on the doorstep and handed him Kate's luggage, so this was the first time that he had actually stepped inside her home.

The hallway was narrow and long and seemed to extend towards a kitchen area past a steep staircase, which must go to the bedrooms.

Kate paused outside a door to his left, withdrew a small

brass key from her purse and carefully turned it in the lock. He followed her inside, but immediately halted at the door with shock at what he was looking at.

It was one of the most depressing rooms he had ever seen.

Despite the bright July sunshine outside on the pavement, the room was dark and gloomy and lit only by an electric light bulb which hung from the ceiling on a twisted cord so that it looked more like a museum or a store room than a functional workspace.

The faint light only seemed to make the shadows darker and he could barely make out what the dark shapes on three large work tables could possibly be used for. Rows of hand tools hung from a rail along one wall opposite the door. Some he recognised from the print works in Boston but others were a complete mystery.

Large transparent plastic storage tubs with coloured lids were stacked three or four high across the floor so that he had to move slowly between the boxes to actually walk into the room.

As he did so clouds of dust rose up and he ran his finger across the nearest work table, leaving a trail in the dirt.

Kate could not possibly work under these conditions. And why was it so dark? The warehouse studio for Katherine Lovat Designs had been light and clean and modern and the exact opposite to what he was looking at now.

'I take it that housekeeping is not one of your strong points,' he murmured, trying to make an effort to be charitable. 'And what is that smell?'

She snorted a reply and pulled out yet another cardboard box from a wide shelf labelled with fading hand-written paper tags, which he tried to peer at but he couldn't make out the words.

'Not a priority,' she replied with a cough, as a thick layer of dust drifted off the lid of the box as she opened it and she tried to waft it away one-handed. 'As for the smell? That's from the leather which is laid out on those wide flat shelves at the back. I rather like it myself.'

'A suggestion,' he coughed. 'Perhaps you might see more clearly if I opened the curtains?' And with that he moved slowly towards the window, but he had only taken a couple of steps when Kate stepped back and placed one hand on his wrist and held it tight with a remarkably firm grip.

'The sunlight fades the leather and the paper patterns—' she shrugged '—and we will only need a few more minutes.' And then she sighed and her shoulders slumped dramatically. 'Ah. There you are. Sneaky little devil. What are you doing with the fuchsia satin bracelet-lengths?'

He folded his arms and stared at her in silence for a few seconds.

'Do you often talk to cartons?'

'Frequently,' Kate replied with a grin, and held up four slim cream-coloured boxes. 'Result!'

'Aren't you going to check what is inside? There might be moths or they might be damaged or something.'

Her eyebrows went north. 'Moths? Through three layers of cardboard? I will have you know that my French grandmother may not have had the finest command of the English language, but she was one of the neatest and most orderly people that I have ever met. Only pristine gloves were packed into Lovat boxes ready for the department stores. There are no moths here.'

'And how many years have they been on those shelves?'

Her hands stilled and she looked up at the stacks and stacks of bulging cartons with their fading labels and blinked as though she was working through the calculations.

'Nana died when I was about nine, so it has to be twenty years.' A faint whimpering sigh escaped her lips and her tongue flicked out and moistened her lower lip. 'Wow. I had forgotten it had been that long.' She looked up at the shelves and whispered, 'I really must do a stocktake one day soon.'

'But not today! I don't think we have enough time,' Heath said between his teeth.

She squeezed her eyes tight into slits and tutted. Loudly. 'Patience is a virtue, you know. But, if it will make you happy, you can take these into the hall and we can check them together before we leave.'

She shoved the slim boxes into his hands. 'I am expecting to see a size seven and five-eighths. White lace elbow gloves and please don't get them dirty. Now scoot. I have three more pairs to find and I don't want to be late for Saskia.'

'Heaven forfend.' He gave her a two finger to the forehead salute. 'I shall be right outside.'

Heath wandered back into the hall and lowered the boxes onto an antique console table and wiped his fingers on a snowy white handkerchief. He was just about to open the lids when his gaze fell on a framed photograph on the wall to his left.

The sunlight streaming in through the coloured glass panel above the front door filled the narrow hallway with rainbow light and he could clearly make out the faces of the people in the photographs.

A young couple were standing in front of a shop front which looked familiar. He stepped closer and smiled. Little wonder—he was standing inside that same shop.

The woman was tiny, dark-haired and stunningly pretty and was smiling up into the face of a tall, slim, handsome man with curly dark hair. His arm was around her shoulders and he was grinning back at her with an expression of such love that it seemed to reach out and grab Heath and force him to look closer.

They looked so very happy.

'Ah, I see that you have found my grandparents,' Kate said behind him and he half turned back towards her as she staggered out with even more boxes. 'That photo was taken on the day they opened Lovat Gloves.' She grinned and shook her head. 'Look at them. Do you know the weird thing? He was still looking at her like that the day she died.'

'He was very handsome.'

'George Lovat was a remarkable man and I adored him. He taught me so much. They both did.'

Then Kate sucked in a breath and bit her lower lip. 'Come and see this,' she said, gesturing with her head back into the workroom.

Heath winced and looked at his watch. 'I don't think that we have the time to...'

She grabbed his hand and slipped her fingers between his. They were tiny and warm and without a moment of hesitation his fingers meshed with hers as though it was the most natural thing to do in the world.

It all happened so fast that his brain was still catching up as Kate marched through the door with her arm outstretched, tugging him behind her.

'That was where Nana sat—making gloves under the window. She said she needed the light for the fine stitching and her sewing machine but I think she just liked to see the garden she had planted. Now, Granddad, he was over here on the other side of the room, at his workbench with all of his leather work tools laid out on the bench. He pretended not to notice when Nana hummed to herself as she worked but we could all see the little smile on his face.'

Her forefinger touched the corner of her mouth. 'Just here. Then we used to giggle together until she realised that she was singing and rolled her eyes and laughed at us.'

Kate's gaze locked onto an old sewing machine. 'Singer, you see. She was singing while she was using her sewing machine, which was made by...'

He chuckled out loud. 'I get it.' His shoulders relaxed and they stood in easy comfort for the first time, her fingers completely enclosed in his paw. 'I'm not sure I could do that. Work with my wife in the same room day after day. Didn't they ever want to rent a workshop somewhere?'

'Nope. They loved being together, working side by side. Each had their own skill and craft but somehow the different types of creativity and different types of customer worked. Nana sold ladies' gloves to the big London department stores so she worked alone most of the time and that suited her very well. While Granddad?'

She gestured towards an old pedestal chair with a cracked leather seat.

'This was where he sat every day. I can see him now, hunched up in front of his work station, a bright lamp shining down on the leather, waiting for him to finish sharpening his scalpel blade and cut the intricate pattern on the lovely piece of leather that he had selected from the wide shelves behind him for this particular piece of work.'

She dragged her feet over to the work table and flicked on the light.

Kate's face broke out into a huge grin and she laughed up at Heath and swung his hand from side to side. 'He loved chatting with the customers who came to see him with their projects. And they came from everywhere. He specialised in gloves for theatres and film studios, so there were wardrobe experts from all over London—and beyond—knocking on the door day and sometimes night. Oh, they were such real characters—but they all had the same passion.'

She leant forwards and whispered, *'Gloves.'*

Then she stepped back. 'But you know all about passion, Mr Big Powerful Publisher.'

Heath peered at the handwritten labels and made out words like *feathers* and *diamanté*.

Tools were neatly laid out next to a modern sewing machine and glove templates hung from a teacup hook screwed into the shelf. Wooden hands stood upright on top of a cabinet with gloves on them. All different. All special. All...sad.

He felt Kate's fingers take a tighter grip around his, as though she had to hold on to something solid and real.

They stood in silence for a second and he inhaled the dust and heady atmosphere of a confined space, which seemed totally wrong somehow for this girl with so much verve and life and positive energy.

*Why did she keep the door locked when all there was inside was a dark, lonely place?*

'Do you live here alone?' Heath finally asked, desperate to break the gloomy silence of the space.

'Oh, no—I have the ghosts and memories of my grandparents to keep me company.'

He couldn't resist it. He had to chuckle out loud. 'Not so useful when you need someone to talk to—or do you talk to them anyway?'

'Wonderful inventions, telephones,' she said, smiling. 'I call upon my friends and amuse them with idle chatter about the silly things that have been happening in the world of tailoring or I go around to Saskia's place and help her with the house.'

'But they don't come here, do they?'

She half turned to face him in the tight, closed-in space

and in the harsh light from the lamp he could see the dark shadows of her cheekbones.

'No, Heath. I rarely invite anyone into my parlour,' she said in a sad, low voice, which had the power to reach out and draw him in.

'Because of the ghosts?'

A faint smile flashed across her lips and she winked. 'Absolutely—they hate strangers barging into their home. And they refuse to talk to anyone except me so it would be terribly rude for guests.'

He glanced around before coming back to gaze into her sweet, lovely face. He was missing her smile suddenly and that flash of her green eyes when she irked him.

'You're quite right. I can't hear a thing. But what do they say to you?'

He could see a shiver run across her shoulders, and instinctively moved closer to give her some of his warmth. It might be a hot July afternoon outside, but the ghosts of Kate's past walked in this room and called her name.

'What do they say? *Katherine, Katherine, why haven't you cleaned me? Why do you keep the door locked? You cannot seriously be still waiting for your parents to give up their scientific careers and make this a happy place like it used to be? That is not going to happen. That ship has sailed, sweet girl. They aren't coming back. They are not. Coming back.*'

The tears were running down her cheeks now and he reached up with his free hand and wiped them away.

Her eyes closed the second his fingertip touched her skin and he felt her gentle shudder ripple through her body and through her clasped hand into his own.

'Are they right?' he whispered, hardly daring to break their connection. 'These ghostly ancestors of yours?'

She nodded, her lips pressed firmly together, and it took a second before she blew out hard and answered in a shaky voice. 'My parents met when they were studying chemistry at university. Yes, I know. *Chemistry.* Apparently my grandmother came from a family of electrical engineers and scientists but the lure of the science lab skipped a generation because she couldn't change a light bulb without blowing power to the entire street.'

She choked on a deep sob which came from deep inside her body and shook her whole frame. 'But I'm a fool. I still cling onto the crazy notion that my parents will wake up one morning and realise that their work in the petrochemical industry is all a horrible mistake and I will fling open the door and they will be standing there on the doorstep with their suitcases.'

Then her eyes squeezed tight shut but Heath dared not speak. She had to tell him now or never say it at all. 'When my grandfather left this business to me, instead of his only son—' she paused and sucked in a breath '—they tried everything to make me sell the shop and move away and retrain in a proper career where I wouldn't be wasting my life on foolish dreams of being a fashion designer. They are ashamed of me, Heath. Ashamed that their child wants to spend her life refusing to conform to their ideas. Which is more than just sad. It breaks my heart.'

Her fingertips moved of their own volition over a cutoff scrap of pale grey suede which was still peach-soft. 'Leather was my grandfather's passion. Look at this piece of suede. Isn't it lovely? Here it is, just waiting for the new owner of Lovat Gloves to turn it into something beautiful. Something to be treasured and kept in a special place by a customer who appreciates fine things. He loved me for who I am and believed in me. Only the new owner doesn't know which way to turn.'

She collapsed on to the stool and Heath stepped forward, their hands still locked together.

'I cannot stand the idea that I would let my grandparents down. It would kill me.'

Heath hunkered down so that his head was at the same level as hers and, before he could rethink or stop himself, he reached up and brushed a lock of Kate's hair back over her ear and lifted up her chin.

'What do *you* want to do, clever, talented lady?'

His reward was a faint smile and the smallest of twinkles in her eyes. 'When I was studying art and fashion at university I told everyone that one day this would be my studio and I would find some way of combining fashion design with the glove-making business that Isabelle and George Lovat created from their passion for the work and one another.'

'Fashion and gloves. In the same shop.' She sniffed and jiggled her shoulders. 'Just thinking about it still makes my toes curl inside my shoes.'

'Then what's holding you back, Kate? What's stopping you from making that dream come true?'

Kate lifted her head and stared into his eyes, her green eyes brimming with tears. 'Life. Reality. I'm scared, Heath. I'm so scared that I'm going to lose all of this that it freezes me. That's why I agreed to come to the wedding this weekend, Heath. I need your help before I lose everything. Can you understand that? Can you?'

And before he could do anything to stop her, even if he wanted to, she slipped off her chair and fell into his wide-open arms so that he could enfold them around her tiny, slim, fragile body, crushing her to him and protecting her from harm with all of the strength that he had.

It had been such a long time since he had held a warm, beautiful girl in his arms, but the instant he felt Kate wrap her arms around his waist, he knew that this was different. Special.

He *wanted* to protect her and keep her safe.

Her hair tickled his chin and he breathed in the fragrance of the woman and the place and the moment, and was instantly drunk on it.

He could sense the pulse of her heartbeat against his chest and the heat of her breath on his shirt and he could have stayed there for ever. Words were not needed. This was the best and only form of communication he needed.

But, just as his treacherous hands moved higher up her back, drawing her closer to him, their silence was broken by a cellphone with a pop song ringtone.

*Leave it,* he willed. *Let the outside world get on without us for just a few precious minutes. Choose to stay here with me.*

Kate laughed into his chest and slid slowly, slowly out of his arms until she was standing on her feet. Still sniffing and wiping her eyes, she flipped open her phone and checked the text message.

She laughed out loud and swallowed before looking

sheepishly at Heath. 'Saskia. Do we want all pink or pink and white balloons? I say pink.'

He nodded, just once, and stood tall as she replied. And, just like that, her body moved out of reach and they were two separate people again.

Except they weren't.

Not any longer.

And he was going to have to add that to the list of things to deal with.

# EIGHT

———

KATE PEERED AROUND the corner of the ornate stone pillar on the bride's side of the stunning village church. Heath was still standing at the front to one side of the altar, working down his checklist and trying to salvage what was left of his carefully worked out timetable.

The late afternoon sunshine was streaming in through the stained glass round window behind his head, creating a kaleidoscope of pastel colours on the old stone floor around him. The florist had come in with a posy of English sweet peas, roses and lilacs to show Alice, filling the space with stunning fragrance. It was going to be totally magical. For Alice.

Heath must have torn up his plan at least three times that afternoon.

He had been so confident when they'd got back to the Manor that they could grab a late lunch, run through the rehearsal super-quick and still have plenty of time to decorate the dining room before dinner.

Unfortunately those plans did not include herding a long line of very merry and alcohol-fuelled guests away from the dessert buffet and free bar and down the country lane to file into the church. He led the band as they staggered down the lane, with Kate and the other three bridesmaids following at the end.

She had no clue who started the singing but the rugby songs were not entirely appropriate for the occasion and Heath's dad and Alice's uncle had to dive in and try to hurry them along, much to the amusement of the friendly young vicar, who was clearly well used to having inebriated wedding parties in his church.

But eventually, with some cajoling from Alice, Charles and most of the ushers, all the guests were seated, Heath was standing next to Charles, Alice and the girls were all gathered at the open door and the organist played the opening few bars of the wedding march.

It was lovely to meet Alice's friends and they were so enthusiastic about being bridesmaids and wearing Kate's dresses that it was easy to get caught up in the excitement and put the morning's trip to London out of her mind.

But that was before she stepped in behind Alice and looked over her shoulder and saw Charles, smiling at Alice as she walked up the aisle towards him, carrying her pretend bunch of flowers at the regulation crotch level. The love and devotion shone out of his eyes like a tsunami which washed over everything else in the room.

This man and this woman. So much in love.

And something inside her had broken.

*Was she ever going to have someone look at her with so much love in his eyes?*

The closer they came to the altar, the more her heart wept.

*Stupid girl!*

She always got emotional at weddings, plus she was exhausted and frayed around the edges.

As for Heath? Heath simply rolled his eyes the minute she had sat down on the hard wooden pew with the other bridesmaids and laughed away her tears with some giggling joke about always crying at weddings.

But when the others leapt up and started streaming out and back to the Manor, she needed to sit in the cool church and gather her wits about her and she was still sitting there half an hour later, watching Heath wander down the aisle and collapse on the bench next to her.

'Well, that was different,' he said and his shoulders sagged.

'I told you that it was a mistake having wine and beer at the lunchtime barbecue. But there are lots of good dry cleaners in the area. They *might* be able to get the ketchup and mustard off your dad's nice jacket.'

'Hah. I would be pleased if that was the only thing to worry about,' Heath replied. 'Did you see the Jardine girls? They spent the whole time talking or texting. I could have been invisible.'

'Let's put it down to natural exuberance and being caught up in the emotion.'

Heath snorted and turned to look at her. He smiled and squeezed her hand. 'Are you okay?'

'Me? Oh, I always cry at weddings and shall probably disgrace myself completely tomorrow by weeping all over Alice before we even leave the Manor. No, I'm fine. Just catching my breath before we start our next exciting adventure—the decorating!'

He exhaled slowly, but then lifted his head and nodded towards his father, who was gesturing towards them.

'Ah. Be right there. But first I have to meet and greet the banking wing of the New York clan and try to keep them apart from the Jardine hedge-fund managers. Wish me luck!'

And he was gone, leaving her alone and bereft while he shook hands and chatted with men who made more money in a year than she would in a lifetime. Heath looked so at ease and confident at that moment. And it struck her hard just how very, very different their worlds truly were.

She had never minded working for a living. Far from it. She was doing something she loved every single day, creating marvellous things for other people to wear and enjoy, and that was special.

Not many people got to spend their lives doing what they were truly passionate about. She was a lucky girl.

A lucky girl who knew what it felt like to have Heath Sheridan's arms around her and to feel the warmth and strength of his embrace melt her resistance like ice in the sun.

The journey back from Saskia's house had been one of the toughest she had ever suffered. Heath had insisted on driving in the July heat and Kate had pretended to doze off now and again rather than face the difficult silence that always came when two people had cuddled who should not have done.

She was mortified at having revealed so much of her past and exposed the tender underbelly of her life. Heath had not said a word. He was too much of a gentleman to make a fuss of it, but the atmosphere between them was so tense that it was making her nervous.

What had she been thinking? Crying on his shoulder like that? Telling him about the pain of losing her grandparents? Stupid, reckless and totally pathetic. And, unless she stopped having these ridiculous feelings about him, it was all going to end in tears—her tears.

Heath was wealthy and handsome and used to the very best of things in life. Why should he put up with second-best like her?

Why should he want her as his girlfriend? Pretend or otherwise?

She was going to lose him all over again. He had his life to go back to in New York and Boston, a lifestyle of wealth and luxury which was on a different planet from the one she inhabited. He was going to leave in a few days and they would both be back in their separate, lonely worlds.

Everyone she had truly loved had left her, one way or another. And setting herself up for even more loss was not just ridiculous but crushing.

She could do this. She was strong. She was going to get through this wedding with a smile on her face and then she was going to walk away from Heath and start living her life all over again.

*Now all she had to do was convince her heart to stop dreaming about the impossible.*

Heath stared into the mirror in his en suite bathroom at the Manor, adjusted the black bow tie below the wing collar on his dress shirt and smothered a yawn.

And he knew precisely who to blame for that!

The girl who had popped notes under the bedroom doors of every guest.

The girl who had cajoled and persuaded even the grumpiest and poshest of stuffy relatives and friends to join in with the decorating operation in the great hall. And not only had they had turned up but they had thoroughly enjoyed every second of it, just as she had predicted. Even the two great-aunts had been singing!

*Singing. In tune.*

And directed and conducted by the one and only Kate Lovat. Organiser. Indefatigable cheer-leader and mind-reader.

And gorgeous. Don't forget the gorgeous.

*As if he could.*

Heath wrapped his fingers around the cool ceramic washbasin and inhaled deeply.

He had let his guard down that afternoon and was paying the price.

There were a few rules that governed his life and one of them was written in tablets of stone and engraved on his heart.

*He would never, ever allow himself to become emotionally dependent on any woman.*

No matter how enchanting and remarkable she was.

No matter how much Kate had touched his heart when they were together in her tiny house. But seeing her tears in the church that afternoon and the gentle way that she had guided Alice into her role—that was something new. That was special.

Kate Lovat was a girl in a million. He could understand now why Amber adored her.

*He was going to miss her.*

In the car driving back from London that afternoon, Kate had fallen asleep in the passenger seat and he had been alone with his thoughts. Going over what she had told him when they had been alone in that dirty, cramped workshop, it had struck him with a powerful realisation that he had never once had the kind of conversation with his father or Olivia that he had shared with Kate in her tiny house. Not once.

Worse—he had no clue about what dreams and hopes Olivia had in her heart or what kind of life she had led until they'd met at a publishing conference.

Perhaps that was what Olivia had meant when she said that he was cold and guarded. And, if it was, then they were equally to blame for keeping their inner truths hidden.

Not everyone was as open as Kate Lovat.

A strange and tantalising thought whispered through his mind and he snatched at it.

His diary was already packed with meetings in Boston and New York for the next few months so this would probably be the last time he saw Kate before Amber's wedding.

He looked into the mirror and a chuckle escaped from the back of his throat and made its way to his lips.

She had asked him what he did for fun. Maybe, just for this weekend, he could take that as a challenge and have some fun, and show her that he could enjoy a party just like everyone else.

Heath Sheridan had just changed his mind. He did need a wedding date, and Kate Lovat was the girl.

He crossed the oak-panelled corridor in four strides and knocked twice on Kate's bedroom door. The latch opened on the other side of the door and Kate peeked out of a narrow gap.

'I'm not ready yet, you pest. Please go away and come back in ten minutes.'

She tried to close the door on him. But he stuck his foot in and then winced as she pushed harder against it.

'Kate! Stop that. You look very nice and we need to talk before we meet the family.'

She pulled the door open, planted one hand at each hip, stuck her chin out and glared at him. 'Are you crazy? How can I look very nice dressed like this?'

Heath took one look at what she was wearing, or rather not wearing, glanced up and down the corridor to check that no one had seen, stepped inside her bedroom and shut the door firmly behind him.

'Kate! Are you trying to give Uncle Harold a heart attack? Put some clothes on.'

Kate flung up her hands. 'What do you think I'm trying to do? Sit there and talk if you must while I get ready.'

Thankfully for his blood pressure and heart rate, Kate strode into the bathroom and half closed the door behind her.

She was wearing a very short silk dressing gown which swung open as she walked. The last time he had seen a girl wearing a bra top, black French knickers, suspenders and stockings had been at a catwalk charity fashion show being held by one of Amber's model friends, who'd found his embarrassment very funny. And he had never, ever been this close to a girl's underwear up close and personal. Amber's modelling work and concert performances required beautiful ball gowns and some of them were a little revealing, but nothing compared to Kate Lovat in her underwear.

Even the girls who came to Amber's sleepover parties used to hide in the bathroom until they were fully clothed.

And Olivia... Well, he had seen a wide variety of designer and supermarket labels, depending on whether she was working on an archaeological dig that week or not.

He glanced around the room and was surprised to find that everything was neat and tidy and meticulously organised. After what he had seen in the workshop, he'd expected that Kate's room would be a mess of clothes scattered across the bed.

'Well, talk to me, Sheridan. What is so urgent that you need to talk to me now?'

As he glanced in the direction of her voice, he caught a

glimpse of the delicious tight curve of her pantie-covered bottom reflected in the mirror and quickly turned away, palms sweaty. She had a waist so tiny that he could put both hands around and his fingers would touch.

He had felt every one of her ribs under the thin top she had been wearing in the workshop that afternoon and the heat of that sensation hit him hard all over again.

'We were so busy this afternoon I never had a chance to give you an insight into the family before we go down to dinner,' he replied after a quick cough, and flopped down on the corner of her bed. 'You've already met Alice's two great-aunts and the cousins. The New York Sheridans were the noisy ones who spent the time arguing about how to string the banners. They will probably rearrange my seating plan at the first chance they get.'

'Heath, you can stop now. I get it. You want me to say nice things and be charming and polite. But my world re-volves around hemlines and shoes and gloves and hats with feathers in them and if they don't like it then they can look at my shoes instead.'

Kate stepped out of the bathroom with her hands still tugging on the back zip of her dress. And his heart stopped beating.

*Shoes?* He wasn't looking at her shoes.

His gaze was locked onto the short-sleeved black dress she was wriggling into. The shoulders were made up of two stiff collars of taffeta which showed her creamy neck and collarbone to perfection.

Apart from a slightly sparkly neckline, it was so totally

different from anything else that he had seen Kate wear that he simply could not look away.

No flashy splashes of colour. No outrageous cutting-edge slashes held together with gold safety pins. She was elegance personified.

He had heard of the expression *drop dead gorgeous* but he had never experienced it before, not even when Amber had invited some of her model pals to a charity event in Boston.

Shame. It might have prepared him for the full-on sensory overload that was Kate Lovat in a black cocktail dress, cream satin evening gloves and a statement necklace which made her eyes sparkle with an even greater intensity than he thought possible.

'Well?' she asked, holding her arms out wide. 'Will this do? I thought about a hot-pink bandage dress but I thought it might scare the aunts and embarrass Alice. So. Black and jewels. Not original. But I think it works.'

'Oh, yes, it works just fine. Wow. I mean. Wow!'

She glanced down at her dress and sniffed. 'Oh. Last season's collection but it was popular. I'm glad that you like it.'

'Like it? I am overwhelmed by it.' And then he realised what he had just said and coughed away her smirk of delight.

'You look perfectly elegant and sophisticated, Miss Lovat. And it's not often I get to say that.' He smiled.

'Well, thank you, kind sir,' and she rolled her eyes. 'Although, I have to say, you clean up pretty well yourself.

Dinner suit. Always a killer on a tall, slim man. Although your shoes are a little boring.'

He stared at his shiny black tassel shoes. Then stared at hers.

They seemed to consist of straps of magenta fabric which went up her legs in spirals. He knew this because she had stretched out one leg onto the dressing table stool and lifted her skirt a little so that she could tie the straps in a little bow at the top. Revealing a tantalising amount of thigh.

*Aha—there was his Kate.*

For a dazzling, bewildering moment he wondered what it would be like to be the one taking those shoes off, one ribbon at a time. It could be fun.

Except, of course, she would think that he had completely lost his mind.

'Did Olivia like shoes?' Kate asked. *As though she could read his mind.*

'No clue,' he replied, then laughed. 'But I have never seen her wear anything like that.'

'Good,' Kate replied. 'The trick is to make us as different as possible. Remember what I said in the car, or were you not listening again? I am Amber's friend from high school who works as a fashion designer and made the splendiferous bridesmaids' dresses. I don't want people thinking that you have been using me to cheat on your girlfriend when she is in China.'

An embarrassed silence filled the room but Kate carried on tidying away her things and organising the contents of a clutch bag, which seemed so small for ev-

erything that she was packing into it, completely oblivious to the fact that she had just dropped a bombshell.

'Good point,' he managed to reply. 'That wouldn't be
fair on you.'

'On either of us,' Kate retorted and shook her head.
'There have to be people here tonight who know Olivia
and would be happy to spread gossip if there is even a
hint of scandal.'

'How stupid of me.' Heath blinked. 'I've just realised
something rather important.'

'You're not wearing underpants?' Kate asked with her
head tilted to one side.

'Sorry to disappoint, but I am wearing underpants,'
he replied with narrowed eyes. 'It wasn't that. I have just
realised that I didn't ask if you have a boyfriend at the
moment. Apologies. I hope you haven't got any plans for
this weekend and, of course, he would be welcome to join
us for the wedding tomorrow.'

Heath glanced around the single bedroom. 'I could
move out of the double and...'

'Relax.' She dropped her hand on his knee for just a
second before going back to getting dressed. 'Stop getting so stressed. I'm between boyfriends at the moment,'
she muttered, 'so this room is absolutely fine. And I can
be a pretend bridesmaid. After all, you're not asking me
to be your wedding date.'

Then she looked up and asked. 'Are you?'

*Damn right he was.*

'A wedding date? Um. Now, that's an idea. How about
it, Miss Lovat? Want the job of fending off all of the lovely

Jardine girls who are gathering downstairs planning their attack now that they know that I am a bachelor again?'

'It's a good thing you are so modest,' she replied far too quickly. 'But I forgot to pack my body armour. Sorry, Heath. I think that would go above and beyond brides-maid duties.'

*Drat. Well, he had tried.* But he wasn't giving up that easily—the evening was still young and there was always the wedding reception.

Kate gestured towards the gift bags dangling from Heath's hand.

'Is that your present for the bride? May I have a peek?' Kate asked and carefully lifted the lid from a lilac-coloured card box.

He was so tempted to reach forward and maybe stroke her leg a little to test that her shoe was fitting nicely. *Bad idea. Bad Heath.*

Kate did her famous mind-reading act again and glanced up at him in surprise as she carefully opened up the tissue paper to reveal a heavily embossed bur-gundy picture album. She couldn't resist peeking inside and gasped out loud.

To his delight, she sat down on the bed next to him and gently lifted the pages. Each sheet was an original hand-painted watercolour with an interleaved protective gauze. 'These are stunning,' she gasped, and blinked up at Heath. 'Wow! This is certainly some present, and what an inspired choice.'

She wrapped the book in tissue and held the box out to-wards Heath, who glanced at it just once and then nodded.

'Alice knew the artist and Sheridan Press employ some wonderful craftsmen who were happy to work over a weekend for a generous bonus.'

'What a wonderful idea. You have gone to a lot of trouble to come up with something very personal which she will love. Perfect. I am impressed.'

'And now for the bridesmaids,' he replied and swung the other bag from side to side. 'They are all different but I thought that you might enjoy this one. Don't hold back—dive in.'

Kate drew out a book bound in pale dove-grey supersoft suede from its tissue-lined box. The pages were ten love poems which had been hand-written in dark purple ink in a cursive font on lovely thick cream paper.

'Oh, Heath. This is beautiful. Any bridesmaid would treasure this for the rest of her life. I love it. Thank you,' Kate said and placed one hand on his shoulder, which startled him more than a little, but not as much as the gentle kiss she placed on his cheek.

His right hand moved automatically to her waist. She smelt heavenly and it took all of his willpower not to linger longer than he should and prolong the delight.

'Right, Mr Sheridan.' Kate grinned. 'I need to pop in to see Alice. And that's it! Time to get this party started. Leave those gift bags to me—you've done the hard work. Fun and frolics, here we come.'

Kate knocked twice on the white-painted door that the housekeeper had pointed out was Alice's bedroom. She had already spotted that Charles was escorting two older ladies down the corridor so she imagined it was safe to enter without interrupting anything.

'Alice, it's me, Kate. Can I come in?'

Alice opened the door wide within seconds and kissed Kate warmly on the cheek and invited her into the bedroom.

'I thought you might have escaped back to London after the mayhem at the rehearsal.' Alice laughed and patted the bed so that she could sit down. 'Thank you for coming back to keep me company.'

'As if I would miss a great party! Gorgeous dress.' Kate smiled and nodded at the pale lilac taffeta fabric wrapped around Alice's tall, slender frame. 'You look fantastic.'

'Thank you,' Alice sighed. 'This is the third one I have tried on this evening. I only hope it works.'

'Of course it will,' Kate replied with a wink. 'I have brought gloves.'

Alice whirled around and pounced on the now clean boxes of gloves Kate had brought from her workshop. She sat back and watched as Alice reacted with delight at the white, lilac and shoulder-length satin gloves.

'Please go ahead and try them on.' She smiled at Alice, who was sizing up the colours and shades. 'All yours to do with as you like.'

'Fantastic,' she replied. 'And I'm sure that I can find a fun evening bag to match. Be right back.'

Kate resisted the temptation to collapse back on the soft duvet cover and snatch five minutes, but that would be far too dangerous. Who knew that hanging balloons, laying tables with flowers, wedding treats and favours could be so exhausting? Thank heavens she wouldn't have to do that very often.

And then there was Heath.

Who had just asked her to be his wedding date.

*Oh, Heath. If you only knew how desperately I wanted to say yes.*

Kate looked around the pretty bedroom with its floral chintz curtains and matching wallpaper. Instantly her gaze settled on a large framed watercolour on the wall opposite the bed. It was a portrait of the Manor with the knot garden laid out in beautiful detail in front of the main entrance with its wonderful colouring and towers.

She shuffled off the bed and strode over so that she could look at it in more detail.

And the longer she looked the more she realised that it had been painted by the same artist who had created the watercolours in the book that Heath had chosen as a wedding present.

A smile creased her lips.

Somehow Heath had found out the name of the artist who Alice liked and had managed to track down some stunning miniatures and flower sketches.

It would be the perfect present and Alice would be delighted.

She was still staring at the picture when Alice came back into the room with an assortment of bags.

'Ah,' she said, and came to stand next to her. 'That's the last of her paintings but I simply couldn't bear to let it go. Lee was so talented and we had such fun that weekend. Charles understands why I hang on to it, but it's hard sometimes to admire the work without thinking back in pain and regret to the lovely friend who painted it just for me.'

Kate blinked twice and her mouth opened to reply but her mind was too busy working through the ramifications of what she had just heard.

It took a great deal of effort but she managed to keep her voice light and positive when she asked, 'Do you mean that this was painted by Heath's mother?'

Alice nodded. 'I know I should put it in another room, but I love this picture and it takes me back to happy times we spent together.' Then she gave a small shrug. 'Most of Lee Sheridan's work was sold in America to serious collectors and there is so little on the market. I'm lucky to have it. But do you know what Lee would say if she were here now?' She laughed. 'Where's the champagne? We have gloves, shoes, bags and the full works. How about we get this party off to a swinging start? I'll meet you downstairs in ten minutes and then you help me open some bottles.'

'I like the sound of that.' Kate laughed and turned towards the door, then paused and looked over her shoulder at Alice with a smile. 'I'll just be a few minutes. See you downstairs. There's something that I need to do.'

# NINE

———

Kate pushed her apprehension deep inside and switched on her happy face as she descended the majestic staircase that led to the stunning entrance hall where the drinks reception was being held.

And instantly spotted Heath.

He was looking out at the cluster of girls who were drinking champagne on the patio, the fading July sun casting a warm glow on his fair complexion and the white shirt. He was leaning against the fireplace, below a set of crossed swords.

A knight of the Manor.

To any of the other guests he would have seemed distant and remote. An elegant, tall, sophisticated and urbane publishing executive who should be on a poster for a classical city boy.

The girls looked like a flock of exotic birds compared to his sober look. But under that fine black dinner jacket Kate knew beat a heart that burned with sensitivity and passion for the things that mattered to him.

But there was something different about his expression. A certain sadness. As though he wanted to join in the fun but felt remote from it.

A hand grasped around her heart and twisted it a little.

She strolled a few steps closer and her eyes followed what he was actually looking at. Not the girls, although any healthy male would be excused for enjoying the view, but Alice and Charles, who were walking hand in hand across the lawns towards them.

Alice looked amazing and the gloves Kate had given her suited her perfectly—which was wonderful. But it was Charles who Heath was really looking at.

The man who had been talking to Heath earlier that day, stony-faced and solemn, was transformed when he was with Alice into someone younger, brighter and happier.

That was it. Happier. Charles was laughing and joking and now waving to the party guests who were starting to gather in the hall.

Kate sighed softly. It must be hard for Heath to see his father with another woman, especially considering what Alice had told her about their past relationship so many years ago.

Her heart went out to him. There had to be some way of making this marriage easier for him to accept. Some way of easing the transition.

Perhaps she could be his wedding date—not for her, but *for him*.

She stopped at the foot of the stairs and slipped into the dining room. The decorations and balloons combined with the sparkling crystal and china and silver-wear to create a wonderful display—and she would be the first to congratulate Heath as being the chief bunting fixer-upper.

Kate walked slowly around to the head of the table and paused at Alice's name-plate, where several gifts were already stacked up on the tapestry-covered dining chair.

Suddenly indecisive.

Heath might not appreciate the little embellishment that she had made to his gift to Alice.

The gift bag swung from her right hand and she quickly glanced inside, clutched it to her chest and carefully slid it to the bottom of the pile.

Exhaling slowly, she caught the sound of the famous string quartet that had started up in the hall.

Time to get some of that champagne Alice had talked about earlier.

It was party time!

An hour later, Kate had found the champagne, sampled two glasses, talked to several relatives from both sides and was now desperate for food and company.

That was one of the problems of being vertically challenged. Looking over the heads of the other guests for Heath was a tad tricky.

Just as she thought she spotted him, one of the Jardine girls bumped into her, almost spilling her drink, apologised and then peered at her for a few seconds before pointing at her chest with a wobbly finger.

'Wait a minute. I think I went to school with you,' the

blonde rasped in a high squeaky voice. Her breath smelt of pink champagne and mushroom canapés and high school cliques.

'Crystal. How nice to see you again after all of these years. Fancy meeting you here.' Kate smiled sweetly. This was not the time or the place to rehash the bullying of arrogant posh girls like Crystal Jardine.

'Yes. I remember you now. You were the funny one.'

*The funny one. Yes, that's me, the funny one. Class clown.*

*Be nice, Kate. You went through all of that at the ten-year reunion. And this is definitely not the place.*

'Well, I did try and have some fun in class,' Kate replied and beckoned a waiter over for another glass of champagne.

'Of course. Christine, isn't it?'

Kate opened her mouth and was about to reply that she had changed her name to Gloriana Hephzibah Wilkes, just for fun, but she took one look at the vacant expression on the frozen Botoxed face grinning down at her with fluorescent white teeth and decided that this girl wouldn't understand the humour and abandoned the idea.

'Well, my mother still calls me Katherine on the telephone now and then when I have forgotten something important like her birthday present, but I prefer Kate. Kate works for me.'

'Kate.' She nodded. 'Of course. How stupid of me. And is the rest of the little band here tonight? You know, the gorgeous lanky one and the plain, quiet one whose dad got into trouble or something? What were their names?

Oh, yes, Amber—she's the pianist, right? Everyone remembers Amber and we are all *so* jealous of that modelling gig she did. But the other girl's name completely slips my mind.'

'Do you mean Saskia Elwood?' Kate asked casually, over the rim of her champagne flute.

'Saskia. That's it.' Then Crystal narrowed her eyes.

'Wait a moment—didn't you used to date Amber's brother for a while when you were in the sixth form? Heath Sheridan. The groom's son.'

A knowing smile crossed the blonde's lips. 'Well, that would explain what you're doing here. Congratulations. You did well there.'

*Well, she had got that right.*

'How clever of you to remember that.' Kate smiled through gritted teeth. 'But I am here as a family friend.'

*More is the pity.*

'Well you must be regretting that. Our Heath is still just as handsome as ever, isn't he? So impressive. And quite the business guru. Perhaps you should have stuck with him, Kate? Or did he move on?'

'Our business interests are so different. I was in London, he was in Boston—it would never have worked out.'

'Really? And what are you up to these days?'

*Scraping a living trying to be a successful designer.*

'I have recently expanded my couture business to include Lovat Gloves,' she quipped, casually flicking off an imaginary speck of dust from her evening dress with her satin-gloved hand. 'Terribly exclusive, of course, but you would be surprised how many people adore having made-to-measure clothing and accessories. Amber Du-Bois is one of my favourite clients. Gloves,' she whispered, leaning in. 'So important to the modern concert pianist.'

The leggy blonde with the pneumatic breasts she had not been born with towered over Kate despite her four-inch heels and looked from side to side before leaning in to whisper in her ear. 'Is it true what they're saying about Amber DuBois? You know. That she had to retire from playing piano because of some unfortunate illness?'

*What? Of all the...*

'Absolutely rubbish,' Kate whispered, 'but on the other hand it's probably not a good idea to go around repeating gossip like that. You never know who might be listening. Heath adores Amber and is terribly protective. Lawyers are so expensive these days. Don't you find?' She smiled.

The blonde's lips twisted with disdain and she simpered. 'Ah. Well, I'll be sure to catch up with darling Heath later.'

'Did someone mention my name?'

A pair of long arms wrapped around her waist and Heath pressed his chin on Kate's shoulder. Kate whirled gracefully around in relief and clutched onto his arm with such force that he actually winced. 'Ah, there you are. Crystal and I were just catching up from high school. Such a small world, isn't it?'

'Absolutely. But I need to snatch Kate away from you, Crystal. We're just about to go into dinner. But we must make time to chat later.'

Heath took hold of Kate's arm and linked it through his elbow so they could glide safely away and out onto the sunlit terrace where the orchestra was playing Viennese waltzes.

'You. Are my total saviour,' Kate hissed out of the corner of her mouth. 'Another minute with the lovely Crystal and I would have emptied the ice bucket over her head.'

'Heath to the rescue. Are you trying to lead me astray, Miss Lovat?'

Kate shrugged and linked her arm around the crook of Heath's elbow. 'I'm your pal. That's my job.'

'And you do it so well.'

'Awww. Thanks, handsome. That's the nicest thing anyone has said to me all day.'

'Seriously?'

'Seriously.'

'Speaking of nice things... I think we are ready for the great unveiling.'

Heath nodded towards the dining room.

Charles had one hand up in front of Alice's closed eyes, then, as the family and guests looked on, he whipped them away. Alice took one look at the decorations, glanced at Charles, who nodded, then looked again in disbelief. And burst into tears.

'She loves it.' Kate nodded. 'We do good work.' Then she hooked her arm a little tighter against Heath, grinned and cuddled closer. 'And I seem to recall that you promised me a dance, young man.'

'Absolutely.' Heath grinned back and extended both hands palm upwards. 'May I have the honour of this dance, Miss Lovat?'

Kate bathed in the heat of Heath's gaze as he smiled

down at her, clearly determined to make her dance. He looked sexier and even more handsome than ever and any resolve *she* might have had to stay frosty and cool seemed to melt like ice.

In seconds they were on the patio and mingling with the other guests, who were finishing their drinks and drifting back in for dinner.

Her senses were so alive when he was close like this. The garden suddenly seemed full of the sound of birdsong and insects. Bees from the roses and lavender were the soundtrack to the beat of her heart and the soft music playing in the house. It was magical. Tonight they sang for her. And for Heath. And only for them.

She simply could not resist him. And it had absolutely nothing to do with the fact that he looked every inch the executive in his superb dinner jacket. No. This was the man under the suit.

*Oops.* She had a vision of Heath minus his clothes. Big oops.

Kate willed down the intense blush she could feel on her cheeks as she felt Heath clasp hold of her fingers and draw her to him.

'Thank you, sir. How kind of you to think of us poor wallflowers. All alone and overlooked.'

'Um. Right. You have never been a wallflower in your life. You look amazing. That dress...' He exaggerated a shiver then hissed, 'Amazing,' bringing Kate's blush even hotter. And with one swift tug on her hands she was in his arms. One hand slid strategically onto her waist, the other clasped firmly around her palm. And her body... her body pressed tightly against his chest.

'Exactly what kind of dance is this?' she dared to ask, her nose about two inches away from Heath's shirt. He smelt of expensive cologne and man sweat combined with something musky, spicy and arousing. Something which was uniquely Heath. A flash of something horribly close to desire ran through her body, startling her with its intensity.

Her back straightened and her head lifted away as she tried to regain her self-control, only to become suddenly aware that the string quartet had a neat collection of waltzes.

Instantly Heath drew her even closer, so that his hips moved against hers, swaying from side to side. Taking her with him. She had no choice but to follow his actions, his broad chest and strong legs pressed so close to the thin fabric of her silk dress that she felt glued to him along the whole length of his body.

'Time to channel your inner ballroom dancing lessons,' he replied, his voice close to her ear and muffled by her hair. And rough, urgent. She was clearly not the only one who was starting to become rather warm. 'Lots of shuffling and gliding and sliding together. Leaning backwards, skipping and dipping come later...although...'

He stopped talking and Kate took a deep breath and asked, 'Although?'

His hand moved sinuously up her back as the pace increased and his legs started moving faster. 'Perhaps not in that dress. It is—' and he sighed, the implications only too obvious as his fingers splayed on the bare skin of her back and his grip tightened '—far, far too tempting.' And without warning he leant forward from the waist, so that she moved backwards chest to chest, both of his hands taking her weight with effortless ease and agility. Except that she had been so captivated by his words that she had not seen the move coming and her arms clenched hard around his neck to stop herself from falling backwards and she cried out in alarm.

With a gentle movement and a firm hand on her back, Heath slowly brought her back to a standing position, his hands drawing her closer and holding her against him as she dragged in ragged breaths of air in a feeble attempt to calm her heart rate.

'Sorry,' she eventually managed to squeak out, feeling like a complete idiot. She knew that Heath would never let her fall. She had overreacted, her body once more letting her down.

Heath paused and released her long enough so that they could look into each other's eyes as his fingers spread wide so that they could caress her skin in delicious soft circles.

His forehead pressed against hers so that his voice reverberated through her skull. Hot, concerned, tender and understanding.

'You have to trust me and let me lead, Kate. Just this once, let someone else take control. Can you try?'

Kate closed her eyes and tried to calm her heartbeat and failed. Her mind was spinning as his words hit home, while all the while Heath's body was pressed close to her, filling her senses with his masculine scent and the sheer physicality of him.

She knew that he was talking about more than placing her faith in a dance partner. And part of her shrank back from the edge. She had never truly allowed anyone to lead her. Not deep down. In fact the more she thought about it, the more she knew that she had always danced to her own beat.

His breath was hot on her face as he patiently waited for the answer which would decide where they went from here. And not just for the evening. He was asking her to trust him with nothing less than her heart. Was he also asking her to trust him with her future and her dreams?

'I...don't know,' she whispered, her heart thumping so hard that she was sure that he must be able to hear it, but not daring to open her eyes. It would be too much.

'Then perhaps I can persuade you?'

Gentle pressure lifted her chin and, although her eyes were still clamped tight shut, she felt every tiny movement of his body as his nose pressed against her cheek, his breath hot and fast in time with the heart beating against her dress.

A soft mouth nuzzled against her upper lip and she sighed in pleasure as one of his hands slid back to caress the base of her skull, holding her firm against him. The fine hairs on his chin and neck rasped against her skin as he pressed gentle kisses down her temple to the hollow below her ear. Each kiss drove her wild with the delicious languorous sensation of skin on skin.

He was totally intoxicating.

The tenderness and exquisite delicacy of each kiss was more than she could have imagined possible from Heath. More caring. More loving... Loving. Yes. They were the kisses of a lover. *Her* lover. And it felt so very right.

Which was why she did something she had believed until a few short days ago would never happen again. She brought her arms even tighter around Heath's neck and notched her head up towards him. And with eyes still closed.

Kate kissed him on the mouth.

Only this was not the kiss of a teenage girl on her doorstep. This was the kiss of a woman who recognised a kindred spirit and wanted, just this once, to let him know how she felt before she lost him for ever.

His hands stilled for a moment and she paused to suck in a terrified breath, trembling that she had made the most almighty mistake.

This would change everything. What if she'd totally misunderstood what he had told her? And he only wanted to lead? Not share.

She felt him shift beneath her and, daring to open her eyes, she stared into a smile as wide as it was welcome, but then his mouth pressed hotter and deeper onto hers, blowing away any hint of doubt that he wanted her just as much as she needed him with the depth of his passion and delight.

A shuddering sigh of relief ran through her and she grinned back in return and buried her face deep into the corner of his neck. His hands ran up and down her back, thrilling her with the heat of their touch as his lips kissed her brow and her hair.

Kisses so natural and tender it felt as though she had been waiting for them all of her life.

Every sensation seemed heightened. The warmth of the fading sun on her arms, the touch of his fingertips on her skin, the softness of his shirt under her cheek and the fast beat of the heart below the fine fabric.

It was Heath who broke the silence. 'Now will you trust me?' He was trying to keep his voice light and playful but she knew him too well now, and revelled in the fact that she was the source of his hoarse, low whisper, intense with something more fundamental and earthy.

The fingers of one of his hands were playing with her hair, but she could feel his heartbeat slow just a little when she chuckled into his shirt. 'Well, I just might. We are talking about dancing. Aren't we?'

His warm laughter filled her heart to bursting. 'Absolutely.' He brushed his lips against the tip of her nose. 'Time to join the others, I think, before we're missed.'

'Missed?' Kate repeated and looked over Heath's shoulder just in time to see Crystal's shocked face staring out from the other side of the patio, open-mouthed. 'Somehow I don't think that they have missed a thing.'

Two hours later, Kate had come to the conclusion that this was one of the best parties that she had been to. *Ever.*

The delicious meal, wine and fantastic birthday cake were followed by more champagne, excellent speeches and thanks from Charles and Alice. Kate and Heath were required to stand up and give short bows for all their work on the decoration. In general, everybody had a fantastic time. Even the snooty cousins behaved themselves. Crystal Jardine actually grinned and meant it and no one started a food fight.

Just as Charles announced that coffee and chocolates would be served on the terrace, Alice tugged at his sleeve and pointed to the presents, which had been stacked on the table behind a chair.

Kate smiled warmly at Heath and nudged his arm as she nodded towards Alice.

But then her smile faded. Because when the gifts were moved, her gift bag was now on the top of the pile and the first present which Alice was going to open.

Kate sat back in her chair and took very tight hold of the napkin on her lap. She scarcely dared to watch as Alice stood up, presented the bag to the whole party and then carefully, slowly, drew out the box, smiling as she went, and then opened the lid and lifted out the book which Kate had first seen only a few hours earlier.

Kate's heart leapt into her throat.

*This was it. Triumph or disaster.*

Alice looked at the book cover with total delight and astonishment and clearly didn't know what to expect, but then she opened the cover; her right hand went to her throat as tears streamed down her cheeks.

Charles looked up in alarm, then Alice smiled and laughed away his concern and, smiling directly at Heath with a quivering voice, she read the inscription at the front of the book to the whole party. "'*To the future Mrs*

*Sheridan. Your love is a beacon in our darkness. Welcome to the family. Heath.'"*

'Oh, Heath,' Alice cried out and, to Kate's astonishment, she put down the book and ran around the table and, to Heath's horror, she threw her arms around him and hugged him and kissed his cheek in a display of open love and affection.

In front of all of the Sheridan and Jardine relatives and friends, who gave a rousing cheer.

Heath was mortified. Kate could see that, and she instantly rushed around and hugged Alice to take the attention away from Heath.

Charles strolled up behind her and man-slapped Heath hard on the back before gesturing for the rest of the party to join them on the terrace for coffee.

It took a moment for Kate to disengage herself from Alice and her relatives, who were gathered around Heath's gift, turning each page in obvious delight.

With total relief, Kate skipped back up to her bedroom to collect her wrap before venturing out into the cool evening air. She couldn't be happier.

She was standing outside her room and was just reaching out to turn the door handle, when Heath stepped out behind her, grabbed her arm and pulled her into his bedroom.

# TEN

———

'*WHY?*' HE ASKED in a voice that was burning with fire to match the fierce intensity in his eyes.

He turned away from her and started pacing, two steps back and forward, then three on the fine carpet. His right hand was pressed hard against the back of his neck as though he was holding it in place and fighting to gain control.

'Tell me why you thought that you had the right to change my gift and make me look like a pathetic fool. Tell me, Kate. Because I really want to know why you decided to humiliate me and I want to know right now.'

Kate lifted her chin and tried to control her breathing. She had never seen anyone with so much suppressed anguish in his face as the man she was looking at right now. She wasn't frightened for herself. But she was for him.

She waited for a second until she could speak clearly, but her words still emerged shaking and trembling in the intensity of his stare. He was glaring at her, his hands clutching onto the back of the solid chair in front of him.

'You knew that Alice would treasure those paintings for ever,' she replied. 'But you forgot something important. Tomorrow is Alice's *wedding day*—the one day in her life when she wants to be beautiful and loved and treasured and admired. But those paintings aren't about Alice, they are all about her lovely friend, Lee Sheridan, your mum. The woman her fiancé loved. And I couldn't let you ruin her happiness by bringing the past crashing into her future. That's not fair, Heath.'

Heath's face twisted as her words hit home.

'Fair? Did she tell you? Did Alice actually tell you how she betrayed her friend with my father when the woman she was supposed to care about was dying in a hospice bed?'

He took a step closer until his nose was only inches from hers, and she could feel the heat of his breath on her cheeks. He was trembling with emotion, so that when he spoke his words exploded into her face. 'Did she tell you that she was sleeping with my father while my mother was dying, Kate? Did she?'

She couldn't speak. It was impossible. Any sort of answer would only make him more angry and upset.

'Oh. For once you don't have anything to say.' He nodded. 'Apparently my future stepmother thinks it is acceptable to share my family's personal secrets and sordid past with strangers.'

*Stranger? That wasn't right.*

'I'm not a stranger any longer, Heath. I'm—' she interjected, but was cut off instantly with a single finger pressed against her lips.

'No. You *are* a stranger. You don't know how hard this is for me. I trusted you. I told you how important it was that my mother's memory was not forgotten. Alice knew her. Can you understand that? She went to art college with my mother and was as close to her as you are to Amber and Saskia. Would you cheat on either of those girls with her husband? No, I didn't think so. And tomorrow afternoon I have to stand next to my father while he marries the woman who is taking over from my mother in his life. That is hard. I'm used to hard; I'll do it. I will survive, but if I have any chance to rebuild a relationship with Alice I have to do it at my own pace.'

His hands thumped again and again onto the back of the chair until she was sure that they must be bruised. She dared to reach out and try to take one of them and calm him and comfort him, but he instantly swiped it away dismissively.

'Did you really think that I would give them to Alice out of bitterness or as a stunt to ruin her wedding day with some constant reminder of what happened when my mother was dying? I hope that I am better than that. No. That album is very rare and special and Alice is one of the few people who would truly appreciate my mother's work. I wanted her to have them. I want my father to have a chance of happiness, but not by playing games where each of us is scoring points from the other.'

'I only wanted to help,' Kate whispered, her voice trembling.

'There is a fine line between helping a friend and interfering in other people's lives, and you crossed it tonight,' he hissed through clenched teeth. 'You think that you know all my family after meeting them for a few hours? You haven't the faintest idea.'

'Then tell me. Tell me why you feel so strongly about one inscription on a book?'

'I don't like surprises and I particularly don't like being ambushed. I never have. And it isn't the first time.'

He collapsed down on the bed with his back against the headboard and dropped his head back and blinked up at the ceiling. 'You want to know about the Sheridan family?' he said in a low voice as though he was trying to control his emotions and failing. 'Okay, I'll tell you about the high-and-mighty Sheridans.'

He looked across at her, his chest lifting and falling with every word. 'Do you remember Amber's mother? Julia Swan?'

Kate sighed out loud and sat down on the bottom corner of the bed. 'Remember? I was summoned to take tea at Saskia's place last month. She still hasn't forgiven Amber for getting engaged to Sam Richards instead of the Crown Prince of some large European country, hell, any country.'

Heath nodded. 'Well, then you will understand how I felt when my dad informed me out of the blue that he was marrying Julia not twelve months after my mother died from cancer. I came home from university to find the staff taking down my mother's photographs and clearing the house of every sign that she had ever lived there so that Julia and Amber could move in.'

Heath inhaled deeply and rolled his shoulders back. 'I

was very angry and extremely disappointed with him for doing that.' He meshed his hands around the back of his head, his gaze locked onto the ornate plaster work ceiling rose. 'As far as I was concerned he had betrayed my mother and I told him that very clearly before walking out and going to stay with my grandparents. I didn't go to the wedding. He couldn't make me and I had absolutely no intention of giving Julia Swan the time of day. And the marriage was even more of a disaster than I could have predicted which, believe me, was quite an achievement.'

'I don't understand,' Kate replied in a small low voice. 'Amber told me that you were a terrific stepbrother.'

He snorted and replied with a small shoulder shrug, 'Amber was a victim just as much as I was. We got to know each other when Julia and my father went on a very long European honeymoon, leaving Amber in a strange house with only a nanny and the staff to keep her company. I went back to pick up some things and found her crying in the music room. I never blamed Amber for her mother's faults. When Julia got bored with Boston and took off for a new lover in London I kept in touch. I think my dad had even less of a clue what to do with a daughter than he had with a son.'

'But your dad has just asked you to be his best man. What has changed?'

Heath hesitated and his gaze locked onto a silk dressing gown that had been left on the bed cover, which he casually picked up and set down again.

'To the rest of the world, my father is a brilliantly successful businessman who inherited one of the oldest and most respected publishing houses on the East Coast of America. Quiet. Intellectual. The kind of man who doesn't make a fuss and likes to keep a low profile, despite all of that power and wealth that Sheridan Press provided.'

She nodded. 'Business profile. Done. Now answer my question.'

'Are you always this bossy?'

'No. Only with you.' She narrowed her eyes and made a point of glancing at a very old wristwatch. 'What changed?'

'I remember the father I used to know as a boy.' Heath took a breath and this time he slid forward on the silk cover, reached out and picked up Kate's hand and turned it over. She tried to snatch it back but he examined each finger as he talked, as though it was the most wonderful thing that he had ever seen.

'My summer holidays were filled with laughter, fun, football games, tennis and swimming. We had the most fantastic Christmas parties where my mother would decorate the entire dining room of our Boston house with fabrics and paint and dad would light a huge fire, make hot chocolate and read stories by candlelight. My birthday parties came with real ponies and trips to the circus.'

'Has Disney bought the film rights for this?'

'Just be patient. I haven't finished yet. But yes, it was a magical childhood that I thought would never end. And, like a fool, I took it all for granted.'

Heath slowly, slowly curled Kate's fingers back around his and held them firm. 'And then my mother was taken ill and it only took six weeks for that world to implode.

Six weeks to make the first sixteen years of my life seem like a happy dream where I had two parents who loved me and a happy home I could always come back to.'

He shook his head and blinked. 'I don't know about your parents, but to me they were the one solid rock in my world that made me believe that I could be and do whatever I wanted, safe in the knowledge that they would always be there for me and for one another.'

A small ironic laugh escaped his lips. 'Wrong. Wrong. Wrong.'

He sucked in a breath and his gaze shifted to Kate's eyes.

Those wonderful brown eyes were so full of emotion and pain that she instantly felt guilty.

He was right. She had no right to barge in and try and take control—not when Heath was still suffering so badly. She didn't know the first thing about his family.

*Only hers.*

What a fool she had been.

As though trying to rebuild Heath's relationship with his father would bring her family back together again somehow. Stupid!

'How did you get past that?' Kate asked.

'We didn't,' Heath replied in a sad but matter-of-fact voice. 'It took me months—no, years, to rebuild my life after my mother's death. But my father was not part of that life. Not any more. Not after his betrayal. Oh, he tried. Many times. But, as far as I was concerned, I had to mourn the loss of two parents, even though only one had actually died.'

A shiver ran across his back and Heath shuddered. 'But he did teach me a lesson. Relying on people for your happiness is doomed to failure. People let you down. People leave and your world collapses. People take away any hope of control you ever had over your life. And I would be a fool to open up my heart and let that happen again. My relationship with my dad has never been the same since.'

'Until now,' she interrupted.

With a gentle smile he stroked the back of her hand with his thumb. 'Three months ago he flew down to New York out of the blue and asked me to come back to Boston to inject some new life into Sheridan Press. I was totally surprised, but he had made the first move. It hasn't been easy to work in the same office but over the weeks we made some progress until he found the right moment to tell me that he was getting married to Alice and to ask me to be his best man.'

'He wants your forgiveness,' Kate murmured as her gaze flicked across his face.

Heath opened his mouth to answer, closed it again and then gave a long sigh. 'He wants me to drag Sheridan Press into profitability, but yes, it did give me one final chance to rebuild some sort of relationship with the only real family I still had left, my father, before it is too late for either of us. And now I don't know where we are.'

He closed his eyes and curved his hands into fists. 'You're impulsive and irresponsible. Exasperating. Never thinking about the effects of your actions. In your world it is okay to ambush other people and expose their feelings.'

'Wrong,' she whispered. 'I know exactly what I've done.

I saved you from making the biggest mistake of your life, Heath Sheridan.'

He looked at her for a second in silence, his gaze darting across her face, but, just as she thought she had his acceptance, Heath got to his feet and started to walk away from her.

She snatched at the sleeve of his jacket and held it firm.

'Alice loves your father and he loves her. But did you know that she was the one who suggested that you be the best man and then agreed to let you help organise the wedding? She did that because you are more important to both of them than you could possibly imagine. Do you understand what I'm saying? She was determined to find some way of bringing you closer to your father instead of driving you further away. And she couldn't bear that.'

'Why didn't you talk to me first?' he asked in a low voice, his gaze locked onto the surface of the table. 'It took me a long time to decide on that wedding gift and I'm fighting to stay positive—and so far all that you've done is take over and snatch any chance of control out of my hands and throw it to the winds.'

Those last few words echoed around the room, penetrated her heart and pierced her soul. He meant them.

'Probably. But you know us creative types, as you call them,' she choked, trying not to cry. 'Total romantic. For some reason I want people who love each other to be together. Call me crazy, but there you are. And, by the way, I know that you love your father. And don't turn away from me like that. You love him and you wanted him to be with you when your mother died. I understand. Truly, I do. But that was then. They have been apart long enough. It's time for you all to go home.'

She reached out towards him and tried to touch his face and comfort him, but the cold shutters had come down and the happy man she'd spent a wonderful afternoon with went back behind the barriers.

'This wasn't a good idea, Heath. I'm going back to London tonight. But know this. I am going to come back here tomorrow to help Alice and Charles celebrate their love, whether you want me to be here or not.'

'What?' He laughed. 'You're leaving?'

'I need to get back to my work and my life without having to worry about upsetting any more of your carefully controlled plans.'

'Your life? And what kind of life are you going back to, Kate? Tell me that—what do you have waiting for you back in London? You're going back to that museum you call a home. Is that it?'

She whirled around and gasped, 'What did you just say?'

'Your house is not a home. It is a museum to a lost world and the people you loved and lost. Maybe it's time to step out of the museum and start living in the real world.'

'Look who's talking.' She swung her arms around. 'This is one of the most beautiful houses that I have stayed in, with a stunning library. But every book is locked away out of touch behind a glass case. Well, I have news for you—books need to breathe, just like humans. In fact, why don't you start here and now? It will keep you occupied until the wedding.'

He tugged both of her hands close to his chest, so tightly that it would be impossible for her to escape.

'I do have a life. A life of my own,' she gasped. 'A life where I decide what to do.'

'Do you? Do you really?' He shook his head slowly from side to side. 'Not from what I saw.'

Kate stopped struggling and tried to calm her breathing. 'Then you don't know me at all, do you?'

She took a breath. 'Charles and Alice love one another and have finally found the courage to declare their love out loud and to hell with the rest of the world, and that includes you. And, unless you want to lose them for ever, I suggest you change your attitude. And fast. Because you need them a lot more than they need you. Talk to them, Heath. Even if you are the one who has to make the first move—you have to talk to them and become the man I fell in love with.'

The words were out of her mouth before she could snatch them back.

*Stupid!*

She was too upset to control her emotions. And now she had told him the one thing she knew that would drive him away. She'd told him that she loved him.

But, instead of pushing her away, Heath whirled around and in one smooth movement he pressed the palm of his left hand flat against the door frame so that the cuff of his fine dinner jacket was flush against her upper arm. Kate was aware that his right arm was high above her head, bracing his whole body on the two hands. Trapping her inside the circle of his arms and his body.

In her heels and his flat shiny black dress shoes, her eyes were on the same level at his nose.

It would be easy to slip under the wide arch of his arm and escape into the sanctuary of her bedroom, but she couldn't. She wouldn't.

His gaze locked onto her eyes, shocking in their intensity. Mesmerising and totally, totally captivating so that it was impossible for her to look away.

And what she saw in those eyes took her breath away.

This was the man she had fallen in love with. This was the man who she had glimpsed that one time before. A man burning with passion and love and power.

This was not the workaholic, cool and introspective man the rest of the world saw.

This was the real man. The real Heath. And she revelled in it. Her heart soared as she looked into those dark brown eyes. Words would not be able to describe how she felt.

She thought that the pressures and struggles of the world had crushed that spark out of Heath and that he had lost that inner spark of true passion.

That long, hard body that was leaning closer and closer until she could feel the heat of his hot, hard, fast breath on her cheeks. He was not touching her. Anywhere. And yet it felt as though every inch of skin on her entire body was burning up in the fire of the intensity of that gaze.

Her skin screamed at her to move forward just one more inch so that her leg could slide alongside his trouser.

He was the golden apple hanging on the tree of pleasure and heady delight. She knew that just one small bite would destroy her—no, destroy them both for ever.

Temptation had never looked so good.

She had never been the kind of girl who could resist the last doughnut on the plate, or the last inch of double-chocolate ice cream calling out to her from the bottom of the carton.

But they were nothing compared to the temptation that was Heath Sheridan at that moment.

He was wounded, hurt, exposed and raw, and in that moment he was truly himself.

She had never wanted anything so badly in her life—not the business, not even her parents' acceptance—came close to the fire that was scorching her whole body and setting it alight.

The hot July sunshine might burn her pale skin and freckled nose, but this fire came from deep inside her, in that locked room where she kept her secrets and her desire and passion.

And then cold reality hit home.

The only reason she was here was to act as a stand-in for the girl who had dumped him.

A temporary replacement. That was all she could ever be to Heath.

Instinctively she stepped backwards to increase the space between them, until her bottom pressed against the hard wooden door. But if anything that extra space made it worse, because now she could see the veins in his neck pulse faster as his breathing speeded.

Kate pressed her head back and bent her knee so that the heel of her sandal was braced against the door. Without shifting his gaze, Heath slid his right leg closer so that the fine fabric of his suit trouser pressed against her thigh.

The sensation of texture on texture was so heavenly that a small half sigh escaped her lips and her eyelids fluttered in a ridiculously girlie act she would never admit to. A tender smile reached his eyes and his gaze released just long enough to shamelessly scan her face and neck and give a lightning-fast glance down her cleavage.

If he was waiting for her to slap him with her clutch bag he was going to be disappointed.

She wanted to hold that face in her hands and tell him how much she had missed him over all of these long years that they had been apart, and how he had filled the emptiness of her long lonely nights.

Who was she kidding? She wanted to drag this sexy, hot, rich, heavy-breathing man she loved by his lapels into her bedroom and find out what his skin tasted like. Her imagination filled in the gaps. His stubble on the sensitive skin on the inside of her thigh. Her throat. What it would feel like to wake up with him in the morning, his body next to hers.

She wanted to know what heaven felt like. Even if it was for just one night.

She slowly raised her lace-gloved right hand and ran a fingertip down his cheek. He swallowed and sighed low and deep, his eyelids flashing closed for just a second.

And in that instant she knew that he wanted her. Almost as much as she wanted him.

Thrilling excitement surged through her. This changed everything.

Torment raged inside her and her brain whirled faster and faster.

Sleeping with Heath would destroy both of them. He might want her now. But in the morning? They didn't have a future together. They never could. They lived in different worlds.

She lowered her hand onto the front of his pristine white shirt and instantly felt a connection to the warm beating heart of the man she loved. She had to be the strong one. Even if it did break her heart all over again.

Tears pricked the corners of her eyes and she opened her mouth to speak but words were impossible. His brows came together as a tear rolled down her cheek.

Kate dragged her hand from his chest, lingering as long as she possibly could, lifted her gloved fingertips to her lips, kissed her fingers then pressed them against Heath's lips. And held them there.

A look of surprise, alarm, delight and confusion swept across his face and his eyes were bright.

Her shoulders slumped in distress. But she did what she had to do.

Kate released her hand from his warm soft lips, shook her head very slowly and deliberately from side to side. And then she pushed him away from her.

As she struggled and failed to stop the silent tears and gentle sobbing intake of breath, Heath leant back and lifted one hand from the door so that he could wipe a tear from her cheek with his forefinger.

The sensation was so delicious that she gave a half sob and rubbed her cheek against his hand.

He looked bewildered and through her blurry vision she saw the passion and fire fade in his eyes. And she already missed it so much that she could hardly speak.

Heath instantly released his hands from the door and almost staggered back upright.

They had not spoken one word in the last ten minutes. And yet she felt as though she had just had one of the most intense conversations of her life. Only with Heath. It had always, only been Heath.

She was the one who turned away, opened the door and stepped outside into the corridor and her own bedroom, bracing the door behind her, knowing that beyond the turmoil and chaos which she had created in his room was a man who wanted her. Body and soul.

*Which probably made her the biggest fool on the planet.*

# ELEVEN

———

KATE BIT DOWN so hard on her lower lip as she pushed her front door key into the lock that she could already taste the metallic tang of blood as she pushed open the door and half collapsed over the threshold.

It took all of what little strength she had left to push the door tight shut behind her and draw the bolts across. Only then did she let her legs collapse slowly under her as she slid down the door and sat down in a heap among the letters and junk mail on the carpet.

She was safe now.

Safe back in her own home.

Safe behind locked doors and windows.

*Safe.*

Her head fell back against the solid wooden panels and she closed her eyes and tried to breathe again. But it was no good. All she got was the complex aroma of leather and glue and old machine oil that filled the air in the enclosed space between the hallway and the parlour.

The day had become hotter and hotter and the air in-side the hallway was heated by the south-facing window above her head. There was no movement of fresh air in the tightly locked house and suddenly she felt oppressed by the stifling heat.

Her eyes flickered open.

She should wash and get changed and have a cool drink. Then everything would be fine and back to nor-mal again.

*Wouldn't it?*

Kate looked around the hall. There were cobwebs under the console table where the telephone and key tray sat and the carpet she was sitting on was pale with a thick layer of dust and fraying at the edges where they were not hidden under the deep wooden skirting boards. The paint was peeling off the woodwork and the lovely Ed-wardian light fitting hanging from the ceiling was thick with dust and dead flies.

She blinked and peered down the hall towards the kitchen and the mismatched china and faded painted cabinets.

Tears pricked the corners of her eyes.

Whenever Amber or Saskia of any of her fashionista pals came around she would laugh off the state of the house by calling it 'shabby chic'. But, seeing it now, from floor height, it wasn't chic. It was just shabby. Shabby and worn and tired and dusty. Just as her grandfather had left it on the day he'd died.

Was that it? Was that why she hadn't changed any-thing in five years? Because she wanted to hold on to anything connected to the man who had loved her so unconditionally?

The tears trickled down her cheeks.

This was how Heath had seen it.

A museum, that was what Heath had called it. And he was right.

It *was* a museum and she had made herself into the curator. As if freezing the house the way her grandfather had left it would somehow bring back the love and laughter and positive encouragement that he had taken with him when he'd died.

She was a fool. The only thing her grandparents ever wanted was for her to be happy, and she had let them down.

Because she wasn't happy.

She was so miserable she could barely breathe.

Her sobs turned into a torrent of self-pity, and she scrabbled about in her bag until she found a tissue.

And then another. Then another, until her sobbing faded away and she sucked in breath after breath of hot dusty air.

She loved Heath. And she couldn't have him.

Their worlds were planets apart and staying with Heath would mean giving up her creativity and conforming to what went for the standards of life in his world. Become acceptable. And it would destroy her. Destroy their chance of happiness. Destroy her dreams.

And she couldn't do it.

She couldn't live like that, even if it meant giving up the man she loved.

He had given her so much. She would never forget him.

Whatever happened, going forward there was only one pledge that she had made on the slow, horrible drive from the Manor at dawn that morning after a sleepless night knowing that the man she loved was only a few steps away across the corridor.

She was going to change. She was going to make her terrible sacrifice worth the pain. She was going to claim her passion—her work—and make it shine by working harder and smarter than ever before.

And that started right here. And right now.

Kate gritted her teeth and pushed hard enough on the rough rug to get back onto her feet. In a second her bag was stowed under the table and she was striding forward through the crates of goodness knew what over to the window above her grandmother's sewing machine.

She didn't need a warehouse she couldn't afford when she had a perfectly good work space right in her own home. *If she could find the courage to clear the space and make it her own.*

Her hand quivered for a fraction of a second but Kate pressed her lips tight together and grabbed hold of the centre edge of the heavy curtain and pulled it sharply across with all of her strength.

She hadn't expected the curtain rail to fall down with a clatter, knocking most of the sewing kit all over the cluttered floor and bringing down what was left of the now ripped curtain with it.

Bright white sunlight blinded Kate with its brilliance. And for the first time in so many years she looked out through the grimy windows at the patio garden, as her grandmother had done. But this time it was different. Because the cloud of dust that had been trapped on the curtain started to settle in the still air and, as Kate coughed and flapped it away, she half turned and saw the truth in the clutter. This was not the proud, happy place it had once been. How could it be?

They were gone.

And she was here.

A vision flickered through her mind of what she could do with the long wide space and she caught hold of it and held it firm before it floated away like the dust.

Kate pushed hard on the window latch. It fought her for a few seconds but gave way with a jolt and she opened it wide. Fresh air and birdsong replaced the dark gloom and she collapsed down on the work chair with a slump.

It took a couple of deep breaths to take in what she was looking at. Shelves and shelves of boxes and bags of dirt-faded fabric and tired, useless trimmings and hand models mocked her great plan.

Reaching into her pocket, Kate flicked open her cellphone. It was answered in three rings. 'Hi, Saskia. It's me. Any chance you could pop around? It looks like I have some gloves to sort out.'

Heath sat behind the library table and picked up the best man's speech he was supposed to be memorising. He stared at the first card, tapping his pen on the desk, but he couldn't concentrate.

Rubbing his eyes, he blinked and shook his head, trying to clear away the fog that came with a sleepless night.

This was it. His father's wedding day. A happy occasion with plenty to celebrate.

And he had never felt so lonely or miserable in his life.

Perhaps that was why he had worked so feverishly most of the night to block out any thoughts except the business. Trying every trick he knew to hold on to control with his fingertips.

But it was useless.

Because all he could think about was Kate.

Heath lifted his head and stared out of the window at the sun-kissed gardens, which were bright with colour and life from the wedding party guests who wandered amongst the flower beds and knot garden after their early morning coffee. The party had gone late into the night but a few early risers were already enjoying the day.

Their happy laughter echoed up to his first-floor window and he smiled back, envious of their easy, relaxed manner. He glanced down at the cards and tried to make some sense of the words he had written weeks earlier in his Boston apartment.

Strange how the lists and charts he had prepared only a week ago seemed petty and ridiculous at that moment.

He turned to the next card, and instantly did a retake.

Because, handwritten in the purple ink that Kate liked to use, was a smiley face and a few lines of a good joke which was so perfect for the audience, and yet he would never have thought of it. He flicked through the cards and, time and time again, she had marked in some witty remark or funny comment which he already knew would make his father smile and Alice laugh out loud.

This was the girl he had accused of being a stranger. And yet she understood his father and Alice better after two days than he did. How did that happen?

Was it Kate? Or was she right? He was trapped in the past even more than she was.

It was almost as if Kate was standing here, teasing him, making him step outside the carefully drawn lines that he had drawn for himself.

They might have started in very different places but in the end they were so similar. Both longing for reconnection with people they had loved and lost, and both struggling to find a way forward and make a life for themselves.

Perhaps that was why Kate understood exactly what he was going through?

He had never felt this connection with any girl before. Amber had been too young to really understand how he was feeling when her mother had moved into his home. And Olivia?

He had never once talked to Olivia about his past, the way he had talked to Kate last night after the dinner party.

He had been with Olivia for over six months and yet he had never told her the truth about what had happened between his father and Alice.

*Why was that?*

Heath raised his head at the sound of a familiar voice and watched in silence as Charles and Alice walked across the garden. His father popped a flower he had just plucked from a shrub behind Alice's ear and then pretended to be taking her photo with a four-finger camera until she waved him away. But she kept the flower.

His father, the romantic. Well, that was a revelation. Like so much of this past week.

He would never have believed it possible that a few days in the company of Kate Lovat would make him re-think everything he'd used to hold sacred.

From the second she'd walked into the London office carrying her box with a bridesmaid's dress in it, with her cute suit and fire-engine-red toenails, his life had been one roller coaster of shocks and delights, one after the other. With him hanging on for dear life.

Last night they had crashed into the barriers.

Kate Lovat had robbed him of a tranquillity and inner calm that perhaps had never been there in the first place, but it certainly wasn't there now.

She had already left when he'd eventually headed down for breakfast. There had been a note for Alice, asking his father not to report that his car had been stolen because she would be coming back for their wedding.

No note for him. *Not that he blamed her.*

When she'd told him that she had fallen in love with him, he had not even tried to tell her how much he had come to care about her. But she knew that he needed her, but wasn't ready to say the words which would open up his heart for pain.

So much for his rule of not becoming emotionally de-pendent on any one woman!

In the course of one week his comfortable life had been turned over and his outer shell of cool disdain swept away and destroyed for good.

She was the most annoying and frustrating and irresponsible and enchanting woman that he had ever met. He was cool and she was as fiery and temperamental as the weather.

Which was probably why he adored her.

It had not taken him long during the night to realise that he had been kidding himself. He *had* given Alice those paintings to show her that he was prepared to accept her.

Just so that he could stay in control of his life, and keep the people he loved close by and safe and protected. People like his father and Kate.

His fingers froze.

Love? Was that what he was feeling?

The breath caught in the back of his throat and he had to cough out loud as the sudden realisation of what he had done hit him hard.

He was in love with Kate Lovat.

Just when he'd thought that his life couldn't be more exciting and terrifying and amazing. And he had never even told her how much he truly cared about her and how very special and remarkable she was.

*Kate was his Alice.*

*And God, he loved her for that.*

*And he had just let her go. No—not let her go. He had driven her away.*

So what did he do now?

If only there was someone he could talk to about the whole mess. Amber was Kate's friend and he had no other close friends.

But he did have his family.

Inhaling a deep breath, he picked up his cellphone and dialled.

Down below in the garden, he watched his father flick open his cellphone as he watched Alice chat with some of the guests.

'Dad? Spare a minute?'

'Heath? Sure. What is it?'

'Something I should have said a long time ago. When Mum died we should have talked it through together like we used to. But instead I pushed you away. I couldn't deal with the pain so we left everything unspoken.'

'I know. It is one of the things I have always regretted.'

'You shouldn't,' Heath replied. 'I'm beginning to understand how love can creep up and surprise you out of the blue. Alice is the only woman who can make you happy and you have waited long enough to be with the one you love. Go for it.'

Charles looked up at the library window and smiled. 'Heath, that sounded positively romantic. What has gotten into you? Or should I say, *who* has gotten into you?'

'Sorry, Dad. Can't talk now. I have to go and persuade Kate Lovat to give me a second chance. You're in charge. But we'll be back in time for the wedding.'

'Not so fast, son. This calls for team work. We'll be right up.'

# TWELVE

———

FOR THE FIRST time in years, Kate threw caution to the wind and turned the water heater to maximum, never mind the cost, and filled her bathtub full of steaming hot water and the scented bubbles that Amber had given her for Christmas.

It was divine and just what she needed to help calm her aching muscles, fevered brain and painful wounded heart.

Saskia had been amazing and, with the help of Charles Sheridan's huge car, every box of gloves in the workshop and all of the plastic crates of materials and tools had been moved out, loaded up and transported over to Saskia's cavernous cellar storeroom. It had been dirty work and, by the end of it, both of them were filthy, exhausted and in serious need of a change of clothes and tea.

Of course Saskia had invited her to stay at her place and be cosseted and cared for and the offer had been so tempting that it shocked Kate with how needy and fragile and vulnerable she had become.

But it was no good, she had explained. She *had* to do this on her own. She had to change her life and make her fashion designs the most important thing in her life.

She loved making gloves. That would never go away. But Heath Sheridan had shown her just how many compromises she had made in trying to hold on to the past. And she couldn't live like that any longer.

It was time to take the risk and make her dream come true or live the rest of her life with regret about what could have been.

The problem was, as she smoothed the bubbles over her now very wrinkly skin, her kind treacherous heart was reliving over and over again those moments she had shared with Heath.

Her skin ached to feel his touch.

Her heart ached with his loss.

Compared to that, her aching muscles were nothing.

An hour later she struggled out of the bath, literally glowing with hot water and bubbles and threw on the first clothing she found in the top drawer, little caring who saw her in her scraggy old shorts and tiny string top.

Kate strolled downstairs, glancing only briefly into what had been her parlour and was now a large, mostly empty space which was aching to be cleaned and reclaimed. There was still a huge amount of work to do, but a smile creased her face as she walked out through her kitchen door onto the patio garden.

Totally drained, she slumped down on the old silver-grey wooden bench with her hands wrapped around a glass of cool water out of the tap, because there was nothing else in the fridge except some date-expired orange juice, and pushed her legs out in front of her to cool off in the shade, a pile of mail and paperwork by her side.

This was her space now. This patio was full of weeds, the once pristine grass and flower beds a jungle of overgrown plants and straggly neglected roses and shrubs. But it was hers. And she was reclaiming this garden, just as she was reclaiming her house and her dream.

All they needed was someone to love them.

This was it. This was her life.

She loved this place so much and she had let it go to ruin.

Frightened to take on such an enormous task.

Frightened to do it alone.

Frightened to do the work and fail.

Kidding herself that she wanted to live this way and would get around to it when she found the time and energy.

*Balderdash and piffle.*

Strange how this garden was so much like her life. She had deliberately chosen to leave the garden pretty much as her grandparents had loved it.

*Just like the workshop.*

What had Heath said? That she was going back to a museum?

*Full marks to the man in the suit.*

Zero marks to the woman who had created the museum in the first place out of a world that had once been so full of life and laughter and happiness. As if keeping the physical things unchanged would bring back the people who had loved her and made her feel special and wanted.

So much for the great, brave Kate Lovat.

Katherine Lovat wasn't brave at all. She was just very good at being in denial.

*Shame on her. Shame on her cowardice.*

She didn't deserve Heath.

*But she was going to.*

Kate blinked her eyes and sat up straight on the bench.

She needed Heath. She wanted Heath. And if that meant fighting for him then so be it. He had filled her dreams and thoughts from the moment she'd driven away from Jardine Manor but it was not nearly enough.

She had a wedding to go to. Pity that she would be spending her time ogling the best man rather than the bride and groom. But one thing was certain.

The last few hours had shown her what she could do when she put her mind to a task.

No more compromises. No more excuses.

Kate dropped her head back and grinned as the July sunshine warmed her skin.

*Watch out, Heath Sheridan, I'm coming to get you!*


'Well, that looks comfy,' came a man's voice from her neighbour's garden.

Kate shot upright and looked around, froze and looked again.

Heath Sheridan was leaning on the fence which divided the garden from the antique dealer's. His arms were stretched out in front of him and a sweet smile played across his face.

She stared at him in stunned silence, her heart racing with the shock of seeing his face. It was almost like a dream come true.

'Heath?' she gasped. 'What on earth are you doing here? You're supposed to be at the wedding!'

'I slipped away for a few hours,' he quipped with a grin, 'to chat up one of the bridesmaids. They have things pretty much under control so I thought that I would leave somebody else in charge for once. I thought that I might surprise you.'

She closed her eyes and dropped her head down with a groan. The next thing she knew, there was a creaking sound and she blinked up just as Heath vaulted over the fence with his long legs as though it was nothing and strolled casually the few steps towards her.

'You weren't answering your phone or your front door. So I decided to take direct action. Don't you think that was rather bold of me?'

'Bold. *Bold?* Oh, Heath.'

Kate looked up into his smiling face and they grinned at one another.

*But she couldn't say the words she needed, so she blustered instead.*

'You have had a terrible influence on me, Sheridan,' she said and picked up the top sheet of invoices which she had brought back from her studio.

'Look at this. I am going to have to learn about spreadsheets and how to do calculations and costings and don't get me started about the Internet auction sites. Why did nobody warn me that they are so addictive? And I only went on them to sell gloves.'

'Sold many?' he asked and perched on the edge of the bench next to her.

Too close. *Too, too close.*

'Lots. Even the pink cotton elbow-length with the seed-pearl trim. Prom-night specials. Amber has been coming up with the marketing slogans for costumiers and fashionistas but Saskia has taken over the actual posting. Apparently I am not to be trusted with combining a customer's address with a glove box with the correct glove in the size they ordered. And she might be right there.'

Kate pressed her lips together tight as she stood up and gathered together her things, suddenly needing to create some distance between them where the truth would not be so hard to express. 'No more locked doors. That ship has sailed, and I realise now that I was only keeping it on because of my granddad. But I am keeping the tools,' she gushed. 'I won't stop making gloves.'

'I expected nothing less,' Heath replied as he followed her into the kitchen, slipped off his smart tailored jacket and leant back against the cooker with his arms folded.

'You're the girl who gave her best gloves to a perfect stranger. Alice says hello, by the way and... What? What is it...?' He looked around to see what Kate was staring at, open-mouthed. 'Is something the matter?'

'My eyes! You're wearing...a polo shirt.'

'Ah,' Heath replied and ran his hand down the front of the pale blue short-sleeved top. 'Yes. Apparently my new step-uncle enjoys golfing.' He looked down at her through his eyelashes. 'What do you think?'

'Think? I am too stunned to think and...what is that? Sticking out from under your sleeve?'

She slapped her hand over her mouth. 'I don't believe it. Of all things. *You*. Heath Sheridan, of the Boston Sheridans. Has a tattoo.'

Heath replied by unfolding his arms, reaching down and tugging the polo shirt over his head.

He ignored the gasp from the lady sitting at the table in the tiny kitchen and turned and flexed his biceps at her.

'The artist was a little inexperienced and we weren't quite sure how to spell Katharine but I think it works.'

The silence in the room was so thick Heath could almost touch it, until Kate exhaled long and slow.

'It does work. Very well, indeed.'

'That's my girl.' Heath nodded and strolled over to the table, reached out and hoisted her onto the table so that she was sitting with her legs hanging over the edge.

In a second she was in his arms with her head pressed sideways on his bare chest. This time there was no struggle or bluster, just the feeling of the girl he wanted against his skin. And nothing he had done had ever felt so right.

'I have some bad news.' Her voice was muffled and she lifted her chin so that she could smile coquettishly at him.

'Hit me with it.'

'Katherine is spelt with a middle letter e. No *a*. Can you stand the pain to have it changed?'

He grinned and revelled in the simple pleasure of pushing her hair back from her forehead with his fingertips as his gaze locked onto her face as though it was the most fascinating thing that he had ever seen. 'Sorry. Did you say something? I was otherwise occupied,' Heath replied with a low growl at the back of his throat, then casually glanced down at his tattoo.

'Oh. The body art. No problem.'

He released one arm, licked his fingertip and rubbed it against the letter, which instantly melted and blurred.

'Alice sacrificed some of her best watercolour pens. I hope you like the flowers and hearts—that was my idea. Dad was responsible for the actual drawing because Alice was laughing too much and...'

She pressed one finger against his lips.

'You tattooed my name on your arm. And you asked your parents to help. I'm not sure if I can take any more surprises.' She sucked in a breath and pressed both of her hands flat against his chest. 'I have to ask. I'm scared to ask...but it must be done.' Then she sighed out her question in one complete breath. 'Does Alice hate me for running away?'

'Alice does not hate you. Far from it. We had a long talk this morning and it turns out that she is actually willing to put up with me to make my father happy.'

'Really? I knew that I liked her straight away. Smart girl.'

'The smartest. And I like her too. But you know what that means, don't you?'

'Lots of family dinners?'

'I was thinking of something more important I have to

decide on first. You see, I want to stop being your pretend boyfriend and start being the man who is good enough to be called your real boyfriend. Do you think I can do it?'

'What do you mean, you want to be my real boyfriend?' Kate asked with a lilt in her voice, her heart thumping. Her blood racing.

'As in stand up and shout it out to everyone in the street and in front of the family at my dad's wedding and for the entire world to hear kind of boyfriend.'

'Ah. That kind. Is that all you want?' she asked in a low soft voice.

Heath lowered his head so that his forehead was pressed against hers and gently, gently brushed his warm full lips against hers.

'I want to be your friend,' he whispered and started to nibble on her lower lip before tilting her head back so that he was taking the complete weight of her body in his arms, and she was helpless to resist the delicious pleasure of a deep, sensual, tender kiss which left them both breathless at the end of it.

'Your lover,' he added and ran the fingertips of both hands down the centre of her back from neck to hips. 'And the man whose smiling face you wake up to every morning.'

'Me?' she whispered as her head tried to catch up with the surge of emotions and sensation that were sweeping through her. 'I am still impulsive and irresponsible. That is not going to change.'

'Good,' he murmured as his mouth found the sensitive hollow beneath her ear. 'And now it's my turn to talk, because you missed out a few things. Such as the fact that you are sexy beyond belief, and I can be swept away by the way you light up a room.'

He stepped back and she instantly missed his touch but he pressed one finger to her lips and, as she watched, the deep caramel of his eyes melted into warm butterscotch.

'I want you,' he whispered. 'For the first time in my life I know what I want and I am not going to question it or overanalyse it. I simply know that I am never going to look at another woman and feel the way I feel about you. You take my breath away.'

His smile spread into a grin so infectious and warm that it penetrated the last remaining barriers around her heart and blew away any lingering doubt.

'I am in love with you, Kate. You are the girl who rocks my world and fills my dreams at night.' He squeezed her hand and looked deep into her eyes. 'I even wrote you a love letter, which I understand is the romantic thing to do. I realise that I shall have to work on my bookbinding but I did have to improvise.'

Heath dived into his trouser pocket and pulled out a piece of white typing paper which had been folded in half and stapled down the spine. A red stick-on gift ribbon had been added to the top and the glue was starting to lift, but Kate stared at it in wonder.

'That is the most beautiful booklet that I have ever seen. But tell me the message. I want to hear you say the words out loud.'

Heath put down the paper, cupped her head in both of

his hands and gazed into her face. 'I struggled with the exact phrase but I know how you like people to say how they feel and not waffle on for ages.'

'Heath. Tell me now. What does the letter say?'

He smiled and kissed the end of her nose. 'I wrote— *Stop talking and kiss me.*'

'I couldn't have put it better myself.'

# THIRTEEN

———

KATE SNATCHED A calming breath and took a minute to cool down as Alice fidgeted on the back seat of the vintage Rolls Royce and checked for the third time in five minutes that the stunning diamond tiara Charles had presented to her as his wedding gift was not in danger of tumbling from her head, bringing the vintage lace veil down with it.

Little chance of that, Kate thought. Alice's hair had been gelled, sprayed and pinned into glossy sleek submission by a team of expert hairdressers who had already been hard at work by the time Heath had pulled up outside the Manor in his dad's car.

Of course she had protested about turning up to an elegant wedding wearing shorts and a strappy top, but he had insisted. She was perfect as she was. He didn't want her to change a thing. And the people who mattered would not care a jot. And those who would care didn't matter. Not to him. Not any more.

It had taken four attempts before he'd stopped cuddling her long enough so that she could pack a bag, *again,* with what she needed from her bedroom. Not that she was complaining. Far from it. She had dreamt of lying in Heath's arms for so long. And the reality was even better than she could have imagined. This was really saying something.

In the end, it had been a mad dash to make it back to the Manor in time to get changed, phone calls flying back and forward every minute of the way. But, even so, she had barely time to hug Alice before slipping on the bridesmaid's dress and matching gloves. The dress fitted perfectly.

As for the shoes?

Alice had chosen the shoes and they were magical. Ivory-and-beige lace, low-heel courts. With a big satin bow on the heel. No stilettos or platforms today. Not when she was carrying the train of Alice's absolutely stunning designer crystal and pearl-embellished strapless oyster silk taffeta extravaganza. She had seen the dress in a Paris wedding shop almost eleven years earlier when she had fallen in love with Charles for the first time and kept it hidden safely away in her hope chest until today.

This truly was her dream come true, and every girl in the room, including the two cousins, Alice's elderly aunt, and even the Dowager Sheridan great-aunt, had simply melted when they saw her in it for the first time. Alice was breathtaking.

Then Heath had popped his head around the bedroom door, which caused much screaming from the cousins, to give a five-minute warning that the boys were just about to leave. He was wearing morning dress, which fitted him to perfection, and her foolish teenage girl's heart just about leapt out of her chest at the sight of him, especially when he gave her a toe to head scan followed by a very personal saucy wink.

That was when the panic started. Four bridesmaids and a lovely bride. All frantic. It wasn't pretty.

Someone slid a fascinator made of feathers and cream rosebuds into her hair, but in all of the rush she had no idea who.

But now here they were. Gliding to a halt outside the tiny stone church where Alice's ancestors had gathered for baptisms, weddings and funerals for generations. Her uncle and a cluster of photographers and guests were gathered in the warm sunshine, all waiting for the bride.

One minute ahead of schedule. Heath would be delighted.

Alice reached out and held Kate's hand for a fraction of a second before she took a couple of deep calming breaths and slowly exhaled.

This was it. Kate gave her new friend a tiny hug and a grin, and then practically leapt out the second the driver opened the door so that she was ready to hand Alice her wonderful, perfect bouquet.

Kate and the other guests sighed out loud as Alice stepped out of the car. She looked so stunningly beautiful and happy that every second of the work of the last few days seemed worth it a thousand times over.

It only took a minute to adjust the short, heavy silk taffeta train before Alice glanced back to Kate over her shoulder and beamed the glorious smile of a happy bride before taking the arm of her handsome, debonair uncle.

Above them the church bells rang out an old tune and, by some hidden signal, the ancient church doors swung open and the opening bars of the Wedding March drifted out of the high arched stone entrance.

With a single nod from Alice, Kate picked up the train, the other three bridesmaids stepped into line and, with a rustle of the heavy silk taffeta gown on the stone paving, Alice and her uncle stepped into the narrow aisle and began their stately way down the church filled with their friends and family, who had turned out en masse with smiling faces to share their happiness.

Bright July sunlight beamed through the stained-glass window above the altar so that the air was tinted with subtle pinks, lilacs and blue tones, contrasting with the garlands of cream lilies, bright ivy and roses decorating the ends of the pews. The sweet heady perfume of the flowers lifted with their every step.

Kate walked slowly behind Alice and her uncle, trying to concentrate on not stepping on the train or letting it snag but the whole time her eyes instantly searched out and fixed on the tall man standing to the right of Charles Sheridan, who was waiting so patiently to finally claim his bride after so many years apart.

Heath looked so handsome as he grinned at her that it took her breath away to know that his smile was not just for his new stepmother—but for her.

Every step down the aisle was taking her closer to this

remarkable man who she had loved for so long. And who loved her in return.

He was her new family. He was where her heart was.

In those strong arms she knew she'd found a home and love for the rest of her life.

*It was amazing what you could achieve in a weekend if you stepped out into the rain.*

# EPILOGUE

———

'KATE, YOU HAVE to stop whatever you are doing,' Saskia squealed. 'I mean it. Right now. Put that sewing down! I don't want you to stab yourself somewhere important. Because I have *news*.'

Kate laughed down the phone at Saskia. 'Hey, calm down, lovely. What's going on?'

'I have just had a call from Amber, that's what's going on. And do you know what that mad woman wants to do now? She's not content with causing uproar in Kerala. Oh, no. Now Amber wants to hold her wedding at—wait for it—Elwood House. My house! On New Year's Day. Kate! This is going to be my first wedding and it is only months away...and I think I'm hyperventilating.'

'Take a deep breath, then another.' Kate chuckled. 'Well, our girl certainly knows how to choose the best. It's a fantastic idea! In fact, I don't know why we didn't suggest it in the first place. A winter wedding at Elwood House. Oh, Saskia, it is going to be fantastic.'

'I know. I've already been thinking through so many ideas my head is buzzing. But there's more. She wants us both to be bridesmaids so I'm relying on you for the frocks. And, oh, Lord,' she gasped, 'I have just thought of something. The mother of the bride. Julia Swan. Help! I don't know if I'm ready for this.'

'Of course you are. And don't worry about the frocks or Amber's mother. We can handle those little challenges. No problem. We are goddesses, remember?'

'Goddesses. Right. Well, this goddess is going to have a little lie-down now before she gets ready to host a business seminar for some accountants. Amber will call you and Heath later! Bye, gorgeous.'

Kate pressed the handset to her chest, closed her eyes and sniffed away a wave of emotion. The first of their little band was getting married.

*On New Year's Day.*

Then she blinked and shook her head. Saskia was right. That was only a few months away. Ah, well, she would just have to fit in two winter bridesmaids' dresses and a wedding dress which was out of this world. *No problem.*

The sound of laughter broke through Kate's concentration and she looked up to see her two apprentice fashion students comparing designs for embroidered evening gloves for an Edwardian costume drama. Katherine Lovat Designs had taken off at the perfect time and an international TV company had commissioned her to create the gowns and gloves for all twenty episodes.

There was enough work for Kate and her two apprentices and more to last for months and the best thing was—it was wonderful work. Creative, luxurious and challenging. She had spent the morning in London museums exploring the original designs worn by the characters in that period.

She was one lucky girl.

Kate sat back in her office chair and looked around the room that had been transformed in only a few months from the cramped space that her grandparents had used into a bright, clean and airy open plan studio. Wide, glass double doors had replaced the tiny windows, and it had been Heath's idea to extend the workshop into a long conservatory room which was filled with flowering plants, bringing energy and life into the long late summer evenings.

Of course, Heath had every right to develop the house as he wanted. He did own it.

Heath had bought the building from her, after all. And the house next door. But they had worked together, side-by-side, all during the summer to clean and renovate the rooms, see its potential and fall in love with the house all over again as they fell in love deeper and deeper with each other.

It was amazing what you could achieve in a few weeks with the help of the right architect and a dream team of craftsmen.

The whole of the first floor of the two houses had been combined into one single large apartment with wonderful woodwork and artisan bookcases created by craftsmen.

Best of all, the antique dealer's cluttered shop and storeroom next door was now the spacious London office of Sheridan Press. Heath had created a modern technical marvel of an office with a meeting room which extended into the garden. The whole atmosphere of his office was unfussy, friendly and efficient and the two professional e-book designers who worked there cheerfully admitted that it was one of the best working environments they could ever want.

Of course, it helped that Heath and his father had worked solidly for weeks to come up with an innovative design for the newly launched Sheridan Press which combined a wonderful hand-bound book with an enhanced e-book digital content which was totally interactive. The awards had come flooding in with orders from around the world.

Alice had made a wonderful new home for Charles in a different part of Boston from the house he had shared with his first wife and they were frequent visitors. But London belonged to Heath. This was his domain, his speciality and his delight. He had made Sheridan Press the success it was and she couldn't have been more proud of him.

*Time to share her news with the man who truly was her best friend.*

The beeper on her waistband flashed out a very private code in reply, which made Kate blush and she slid from her chair and strolled over into the garden room.

Heath Sheridan was leaning on the small white-painted wooden gate, which separated the two houses, with a big cheesy grin on his face.

Kate slid open the glass doors and stepped out into the early September air.

She reached up with both hands to take his face, tilted

her head and kissed him with all the warmth and tenderness in her body. His reply was to kiss her back hard enough to make her toes tingle and her knees melt.

'Hi, handsome,' she said, getting her breath back. 'What's new?'

'Oh, the usual.' He smiled and, in a pretend serious voice, said, 'More awards, more orders, more news from Boston.' Then he grinned. 'How about you?'

'Amber is coming home for New Year and has decided to get married at Elwood House. Many new frocks and gloves will be needed. But I wonder who she could possibly ask to help organise the event. Any ideas?'

His reply was to press his lips against hers. 'None at all,' he whispered. 'Because I am fully booked, and I am going to stay booked for a very, very long time.'

\* \* \* \* \*

*Look for Saskia's story in*
*BLAME IT ON THE CHAMPAGNE*
*Coming soon*

Heidi Rice brings you another story in
The Wedding Season miniseries with

# MAID OF DISHONOR

"You wanna know the one thing I remember real clear from that night?" he murmured.

She shook her head, knowing she didn't want to know, especially not in that low, seductive growl that was setting sparks off all over her sex-starved body.

"However wrong we were for doing it, it felt right while it lasted."

Her pulse rate accelerated at the forceful tone. "I don't think we should talk about that," she whispered, her voice faltering along with her resistance. "It's a really bad idea."

He climbed off his stool and pressed his hand to her back—making the tingles hit meltdown as he rubbed the slinky silk over sensitized skin. He hooked her hair behind her ear and leaned in to whisper against her lobe, "Bad ideas can lead to awesome sex."

She shuddered, not caring anymore that she was sitting in a public bar or that she wanted to stretch against his palms like a contented cat.

"And it's not wrong anymore," he murmured, his breath hot and seductive against her ear.

She raised her head. "Are you sure about that?" she said a little breathlessly, as it occurred to her just how far removed the Carter who stood before her now was from the innocent man she'd once seduced, if that cocksure look was anything to go by.

"I'm not dating right now. Are you?" he said, deliberately misinterpreting the question.

"No, but…"

He pressed a thumb to her lips, silencing the feeble protest.

"Didn't you ever wonder what it would be like between us…without all the emotional garbage tripping us up?"

*Emotional garbage.*

She heard the words and saw the harsh cynicism behind the hunger.

"Yes, I have," she answered honestly, because there wasn't much point being coy when her desire had outstripped her caution a good half an hour ago.

Was she seriously considering this? And why couldn't she seem to consider anything else, such as running off screaming into the night, which had to be the smarter, safer, more sensible option?

He placed both his hands on her waist and drew her off the stool until she stood in his embrace, that spicy, musky scent intoxicating her. "I have a whole hotel suite upstairs, if you want to find out the answer."

**Pick up MAID OF DISHONOR by Heidi Rice, on sale August 20, 2013, wherever Harlequin® books are sold.**

# New York. New guy.
## *New Kelly!*

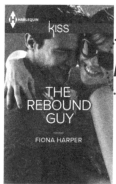

## THE REBOUND GUY...
Fiona Harper

After Kelly Bradford's past few years, all she wants is a steady life. She certainly doesn't need the hassle of men or dating after everything she's been through. So she absolutely, categorically should *not* be fantasizing about Jason Knight—her boss...and a man whose very smile screams trouble!

But a business trip to New York pushes her resolutions to the max—the adrenaline of the Big Apple has nothing on the excitement Kelly feels around Jason! Maybe a rebound fling is just what she needs to make her feel alive again....